Jack Kerouac is Dead to Me

Jack Kerouac is Dead to Me

Gae Polisner

WEDNESDAY BOOKS
NEW YORK

First published in the United States by Wednesday Books,
an imprint of St. Martin's Publishing Group

JACK KEROUAC IS DEAD TO ME. Copyright © 2020 by Gae Polisner.
All rights reserved. Printed in the United States of America.
For information, address St. Martin's Publishing Group,
120 Broadway, New York, NY 10271.

www.wednesdaybooks.com

Designed by Anna Gorovoy

The Library of Congress Cataloging-in-Publication Data is available
upon request.

ISBN 978-1-250-31223-5 (hardcover)
ISBN 978-1-250-31225-9 (ebook)

Our books may be purchased in bulk for promotional, educational,
or business use. Please contact your local bookseller or the Macmillan
Corporate and Premium Sales Department at 1-800-221-7945, extension 5442, or by e-mail at MacmillanSpecialMarkets@macmillan.com.

First Edition: April 2020

10 9 8 7 6 5 4 3 2 1

33614081699927

To all the girls and women who
stand by one another without judgment,
who support one another and lift each other up.

And, to all those who continue to lift me up, too.

Suffer me to take your hand.
Suffer me to cherish you
Till the dawn is in the sky.
Whether I be false or true.

"MARIPOSA," EDNA ST. VINCENT MILLAY

NOW. JUNE 29.
MALIBU, CA

Aubrey,

I've started this letter three times, but each place I begin feels wrong. I get lost in the memories and my thoughts lose their way, and I have to start over again. But, as hard as it is to find my way in, I know I need to try. I have to figure out why we hurt each other the way we did, how we ended up hating each other so much.

Sometimes, I miss you so bad I can't breathe, and I break down in tears, or get so mad at you I wonder why I even care. But, in my heart, I know why I do. You were always my best friend, Aubrey, the one person who understood.

I hope you will understand now.

Part I

We most often observe butterflies hovering amidst gardens, but some may be found in mud puddles; there are valuable nutrients to be gained there, too.

LATE JUNE
BEFORE EIGHTH GRADE

The day is hot. We're running through the sprinkler in my backyard, dodging in and out of the cold spray that fans over us, shrieking as droplets rain down onto our sun-warmed, tanned skin.

You push me closer as the arc of water returns, and I fall onto the grass, wet, laughing, taking you down with me. The sod under us is new and soft, and the freshly cut blades stick to our limbs, our faces.

We are giddy with summer, with each other. We are still on the cusp of everything.

Afterwards, you turn off the hose, and we lie on faded chaise lounges we drag to the middle of my yard, our chests heaving with rapid, satisfied breaths in our barely-filled-out bikini tops.

You reach out and take my hand and an indescribable sort of electricity shoots through me, real and palpable, as if I could reach out the fingers of my other hand and touch it, some white-hot charge that holds us together.

We are friends—best friends—but more than that. We are entirely, platonically, in love.

"See that cloud, JL?" You let go and point off beyond the top of the tallest sycamore branches. "It looks like a giant mushroom, doesn't it?" My eyes follow your finger, my hand cold from the loss. "Do you see it there?"

I bust out laughing.

"What's so funny?" you ask, your voice defensive.

I lean all the way over, tilt your face a bit with my hand to change the angle. "It looks a lot like something else, Aubs. Look again."

You sit up and squint to see clearer. After a second, you say, "Oh my god, it's a giant penis cloud, isn't it?" and we both fall apart laughing.

When our stomachs hurt so bad we have to fight from laughing more, you lie back down and ask softly, "Have you ever seen one for real, JL?"

"A penis? No." I think for a minute. "I mean, pictures, yes, but not in real life, in person. Why? You?"

You nod and look at me, eyes big, mouth covered by your own hand like you've revealed some dangerous secret, making me sit up and demand, "Okay, spill! Whose?" You shake your head hard, your eyes round over your still-cupped fingers. I run off a few names, guessing.

"David Brundage?"

"Scott Silvestri?"

"Matthew Flynn?"

You uncover your mouth. "God, no! I hear it's giant, though. Like a grown man's . . ."

"Well, tell, then."

"No one from school," you say, covering your mouth again and adding through half-open fingers, "closer to home, JL. Come on."

"Ew, Ethan's?" I squeal too loudly, and you nod, and we both shriek and shudder in exaggerated, disgusted delight. "Oh my god!" I say. "Why?"

"By accident, obviously. I wasn't trying! I walked in on him in the bathroom. He forgot to lock the door, and—"

"Ew! So gross! Don't tell me!" I cry, but I have a thousand questions. Ones I will never dare ask.

"Right? Totally. That thing is, like, burned into my brain!" We shudder one more time for good measure.

After, we're quiet for a while, and the clouds shift and the mushroom one feathers out and disappears.

I take your hand this time, feeling the electric bond return as I swing our clasped fingers together in the space between our chairs.

"I love you," I say.

"Me too," you respond too quickly. I roll my head to the side and smile, and you add, "Your boobs are getting bigger than mine. No fair."

"They are?" I glance down my chest toward my two pathetic, barely-there mounds beneath the bikini fabric.

You nod. "Yes. And you're so pretty—too pretty—you're really perfect, you know? I've never had a friend as perfect as you."

It should be a compliment but, instead, the electricity fizzles as if short-circuited, and my chest fills with an inexplicable sense of dread. Your admiration feels somehow fragile and conditional, and impossible to live up to.

"No I'm not, don't be stupid," I say, irritated. I want to untangle my fingers, get up, and sprint across the lawn, but you squeeze harder to hold on.

"Yes you are. Admit it."

"Aubs—"

"Well, I think you are. I wish I were more like you. Pretty and free, and not afraid of anything, like your mother."

It feels worse when you add this, because you don't know me if you think I'm like her. I'm nothing like her, off-kilter and unfettered, nor half as beautiful. I'm plain, but I'm solid. And, yet, it isn't about me, suddenly. It's what you have decided. You have judged me as one thing, and at some point, I will disappoint you by proving you wrong.

"I am not," I say again, to right things.

"Are too," you insist, making my face redden in protest. But you don't notice. You don't see. And even if you turned and looked at me, you couldn't tell the flush of anger in my cheeks from too much sun. "I just wish I could be more like you. Geesh, that's all."

"You do?"

You nod, and squeeze my fingers even harder, and we both close our eyes. I leave them there in yours even though a few are starting to go numb.

"So much," you say.

"Really?"

"Yes. Really."

So, maybe I'm wrong.

Maybe you're not judging me at all.

I squeeze back, letting go of my unease, wanting to hold on to whatever spell has you enamored with me, instead.

Or maybe I'm weak and don't have the heart to call out the lie, and tell you how afraid of everything I really am.

MID-APRIL
TENTH GRADE

I move the bent paper clip loop toward the butterfly's abdomen, my thumb and forefinger pressed gently on her wings to steady her. My eyes dart nervously to the image paused on my laptop screen, and my hand trembles.

I stop.

I can't do it.

These kinds of videos always lie. They make it seem easy when it isn't. And when you try it yourself, it never works like the guy on the screen said it would. There's no way pinning this poor creature down like this won't kill her. But she's as good as dead with this break in her wing, so it's either this or do nothing and watch her struggle and die.

I press play, wishing Aubrey were here to calm me, trying not to glance at the photo of Mom and Dad and me together on the shelf above my desk. Smiling after eighth-grade graduation.

A lot can change in more than a year. And he originally promised he'd be back in six months.

"End of May, sweetheart," he promised again last week. "Less than six weeks left to go." But how many times in the past eighteen months had I heard that?

"By fall, JL, I promise."

"By Christmas."

"Just a few more weeks."

Then, the inevitable phone call, and the same old explanation that the company still needs him, that there are options in his contract he can't avoid.

Followed by more of Mom's tears, and her slipping further and further into oblivion.

I move the cursor back to the beginning and hit play again. The video starts over and I try to focus on the man's calm English accent as he moves me through the instructions: "Use the paper clip to gently restrain the butterfly around its abdomen . . . now that you have it immobilized . . . use your toothpick to dab a dot of glue over the break site . . ." Like it's no big deal that I will kill the poor thing if I mess up. Like he's explaining how to fix a flat tire.

Shit.

I take a deep breath, fighting the inclination to close my eyes. I'd better move faster. I'm already too far behind. I press the metal loop down over her abdomen, and her wings pulse instinctually—once, twice, against the restraint like a heartbeat.

". . . glue over the surface of the cardboard splint . . . dry a minute or two to set. Now, using your tweezers, and making sure the wing is lined up perfectly, carefully place your card stock splint over the fractured area . . . no ability to redo, so take your time . . . dusting powder gently over the wing to counteract excess glue."

Is he kidding me going so fast?

I need to pause the video, but don't have a hand free, so I plow forward, coaching myself aloud. "You've watched it four times, JL. You've got this. You already know what to do."

I'm shaking so badly, I whisper the steps aloud: "Glue. Splint. Powder. Breathe. And you're done."

"When the glue is dry," he says, "gently remove the butterfly from the cloth surface. It may even be stuck . . . release it free. It's good to go!"

It moves on to the next video, *Twenty Child Stars You Didn't Know Passed Away,* and I haven't even dabbed the glue yet.

I take my time, ignoring the noise in the background, as I move the small cardboard splint to its wing. I place the splint gently down over the break and sprinkle some powder from the bottle.

Voila! Right?

I lift the metal loop and wait.

The poor creature doesn't move at all.

Tears spring to my eyes. I should have known better than to try to fix anything.

I slam my laptop shut, chuck the mangled paper clip in the wastebasket, and lie back onto my bed, wishing Max were here. Max, not Aubrey. Aubrey has made her intentions perfectly clear.

She prefers those other girls now.

The phone rings down the hall, and I wait to hear if Mom will get it, but she rarely does. Maybe she's not even home from her appointment with Dr. Marsdan yet. She's up to two or three times per week with him.

I roll onto my side, fighting the urge to call Max. He's at work and I don't want to bother him. My stomach flutters. I still can't believe I'm dating Max Gordon.

The phone rings again. Only Dad and Nana still call our landline, and Dad barely does. It's probably a sales call, some scammer pretending to be from the IRS.

If it's Nana, I'll call her back. I'm not in the mood for her, or to tell her I already lost one of the butterflies. It's not that I don't love her. I do. But I'm tired of her head-in-the-sand cheerfulness, the way she deflects and pretends, acting like everything with Mom is okay. Shooing away the truth like some pesky fly.

"It's only a rough spell, honey. Your mother has always been given to histrionics, even as a girl. She'll be fine. And Dr. Marsdan is the best. He helped my friend Marcy's daughter. She's good as new. He'll fix her in no time. Plus, everything will be better when your father gets home."

My eyes shift to my desk, to the photo, to my open laptop, to the mess of glue and cotton balls and underneath. To the habitat Max helped me put together a few short weeks ago. The day Aubrey was last here, the day the larvae arrived. And the last time we made any pretense of hanging out.

She made it clear what she thought of me that day. The minute she said that stupid thing about the Jezebels.

LATE MARCH
TENTH GRADE

I unpack the box from *World of Butterflies*—the cultures, the clamp lamp, the reagents and plants Nana and I ordered for the caterpillars to snack on—leaving all sorts of labels and pamphlets and instruction sheets strewn about my bedroom floor, and gently lift the two small remaining boxes out, one marked *Greta oto/Glasswings,* the other *Delias hyparete/Painted Jezebels.* I place them on the floor in front of us.

"What are these?" you ask, picking up the first box too aggressively. I take it back from you.

"Glasswings, Aubs," I say. "And the others are Painted Jezebels. Wait till you see how cool they are."

You think I don't notice how you roll your eyes before you get up and lie back on my bed, your cell phone held above you in the air. You're texting fast. A group chat that obviously doesn't include me.

I could ask who, but I know. Instead, I focus on lining up the culture cups next to the boxes of larvae, which will be tiny and weird, since they're only in their first or second instar phases.

You used to care about this stuff, too, think it mattered. You used to be interested in all the research I did to help them emerge. Now it's beneath you, or something.

I try not to feel bad, look to Max for some sort of enthusiasm or support, but he's oblivious, sitting hunched at my desk, head down, singing, and concentrating on assembling the habitat.

"Blue-eyed son . . . darling young one." He suddenly sings out loud, too loud, his muscles flexing under his plain white T-shirt, his head bobbing to whatever song he has blaring enough that I can hear it through the earbuds. Some piece of classic rock, not far from the type of stuff my dad listens to, or would listen to if he were still home.

"Tongues were all broken . . . guns . . . swords . . ." Max sings, dropping every few words, others lifting awkwardly into the air, which makes you glance up and roll your eyes again, before returning to your oh-so-important texting.

Why are you even here, Aubrey? I want to ask, but I don't want to make things worse. Besides, it doesn't matter what you think. I love it when Max sings, especially when it seems like he's singing to me, his deep, raspy voice breaking through like he doesn't give a crap what anyone thinks of him.

Not you. Not me. Not anyone.

I turn back to you, and watch you watching him.

"What?" you finally ask, and I give you a look.

"Nothing. It's . . . I'm stressed about this, Aubs." I motion at all the packages, the equipment, the moving parts I have to get right if I want these boxes of larvae to turn into full-blown tropical butterflies in a matter of weeks. "At least *he's* helping. I thought you were going to help. *Wanted* to help. I thought you were excited."

"I was," you say, adding defensively, "I mean, I *am.*" You type something else fast, before swinging your legs around the side of the bed to sit up. "Plus, I offered to help last night, remember? After the mall. But some of us were too busy to go."

But you knew when you invited me I wasn't going to. You knew I wouldn't be comfortable hanging with those girls or, worse, being stuck inviting them over here after. Not with Mom the way she can be. *Is.* Not until she's doing better. There are people you can risk things with, and people you can't.

"But, seriously, JL," you say, lowering your voice, "I'm still not sure what you see in him."

Liar, Aubrey!

Sorry, but you are. Whatever people had to say about Max Gordon, or thought they knew about him, he is undeniably hot, and undeniably good with his hands. Not like you're thinking, either—I'm not saying that. But he can __make__ anything, fix anything. Build dirt bikes from scraps. Play guitar.

People underestimate how smart he is, too. His mother is an English teacher, so he's read all sorts of books. More than I ever will. More than you. All the classics, and famous poems, lines he can recite by heart. So if he wasn't Mr. Honor Society, maybe it's because he didn't want to be. Maybe he didn't give a crap about that kind of thing . . .

And that day the Tropicals arrived? I was happy, Aubrey, happy about Max, about us being a couple, and all I wanted was for you to be happy for me, too.

But you weren't, were you? You weren't even willing to try.

I don't answer you. I won't justify your jealousy, or whatever it is, by defending Max Gordon. At least you slide back onto the floor as if you might be ready to help me. I hand you the cup with the Jezebel larvae.

"Ew, gross," you say, peering in.

"They're not gross. They're cute."

I look into the other culture that holds several tiny brownish-yellow worms with pin-sized black heads. It's the first time I'm raising butterflies from this early larval phase, and, yeah, they're definitely not as cute as the full-grown Monarch or Swallowtail caterpillars, with their yellow and black stripes and little Muppet-looking faces.

"Wait till you see them hatch," I say. "They're ridiculously pretty. And these," I add, holding out the cup with the Glasswing larvae, "the chrysalises are this amazing iridescent, neon green, like a gemstone, and the butterflies are totally transparent."

"Like glass," you say, and I can't tell if you're being sarcastic. You tip the culture cup you're holding at me, and think for a second. "And these? Why are they called Jezebels, anyway?" Panic rises in my chest before I even know why, because there's something in your voice, something cruel, even if you're pretending the question is innocent. It's as if you've been waiting to ask it. "*Jez-e-bels*," you repeat purposefully, emphasizing all three syllables.

"I don't know, Aubs; why?" I swallow hard. "Why would I care?"

"No reason. It's just, I asked my mom one day, because you had been talking about the butterflies, you know, 'Jezebels this, and Jezebels that,' and she was watching one of those old black-and-white movies she loves, and when the commercial break was over and the title came on—get this—guess what it was called?"

"*Jezebels*," I snap back, annoyed.

"*Jeze*bel, singular, actually. But, I mean, what are the chances of that?"

"I have no idea," I say.

"Anyway, I asked my mom what the film was about, because it's such a coincidence, right? And she said it was about this skanky Southern belle who everyone thinks is a whore. Because that's what a Jezebel is, JL. A Jezebel is a whore. And it's just kind of odd that, of all the butterflies you could have picked—"

My eyes shoot to you, my throat lodging with tears. "We both know your mother didn't say that," I challenge, because there's not a chance in hell Mrs. Andersson used any of those words.

"Not directly . . . but she made it clear." Your eyes laser focus on me and you add, "I'm trying to help, JL. That's all I'm doing." You shift your gaze from me to Max, and back to me. "Like, you know he's nineteen, right? And not exactly—"

"Of course I do!" I cut you off. "You're being stupid is what you're doing." I fight to keep my voice from breaking. I don't want to give you the satisfaction. Besides, Max and I haven't been dating that long. We haven't done much. I haven't done *anything*. "Why don't you go, Aubrey?" I say, standing. "It's obvious you don't want to be here."

You stand, too. "I'm just saying, JL, if you talk about them in public—the butterflies, I mean—the name is kind of suggestive. So, maybe don't call them that, is all."

"Noted."

You move to my bedroom door, and I hold it open for you, half-hoping you'll argue, say you're sorry, that you really want to stay. You hover there, wordless.

"All set, Jailbait!" Max exclaims too loudly, before yanking his earbuds out and tossing them onto my desk. He stands, nearly knocking my desk chair over with his strong, solid body, and stretches, causing his white T-shirt to ride up, revealing the edge of a sleek black motorcycle tattoo peering from the waistband of his jeans. I've traced my finger along its outline, asking questions, but all I really know is that he put it there, hidden, because his dad would "kick my ass otherwise." He turns to me and says, "One deluxe butterfly habitat, fully assembled, though it wasn't much more than screwing a few screws."

(I feel your eyes bore through the back of my head.)

Max kicks the cardboard and Bubble Wrap away from the leg of the chair with his work boot–clad foot, and places the multi-level habitat on the floor. He scans the room, confused, and raises his eyebrows at my open door, but I don't turn.

"What happened?" he asks. "Where'd she go?"

I don't answer.

It's better at this point if you've gone.

SEPTEMBER
FIFTH GRADE

1. *Always be friends.*
2. *Never fight.*
3. *Never <u>ever</u> date a boy the other person likes.*
4. *Never keep secrets from each other.*

You put your pen down.
"Anything you want to add?" you ask.

My cell phone buzzes from my desk, next to the dead, splinted Jezebel and my closed, unhelpful laptop.

"Shut up," I say, as it vibrates against the wood, but what if it's Max?

I still can't bring myself to answer it.

I close my eyes. *Poor, dead butterfly.*

From the larvae that shipped, only half survived through the fifth and sixth instar phase, and of those, only seven butterflies had emerged from their beautiful chrysalises. Three Glasswings and four Jezebels, that's it. I had already felt like a failure, and now one of the Jezebels is dead.

Aubrey would be pleased. Not including me, one less Jezebel in the world.

My phone buzzes again—this time a brief, single message alert—so I force myself over to my desk to clean up. But when I get there, the butterfly is upright, her wings folded back and her antennae poking about in the air.

I know she's only a butterfly, but I'm so happy I could cry.

I watch, overwhelmed, as she crawls to the edge of my desk, her proboscis dipping, her wings preparing for flight. She takes off, circling the room a few times before she lands on the habitat, next to the orange slice I placed there.

I give her a moment to drink, before lifting her with the fruit and slipping her carefully back inside.

On my cell, the message is from Dad. My chest tightens. What if he's changing his plans? I dial him back, my heart sinking, but it rings four times, and goes to voicemail.

Maybe that's best. Maybe I don't want to know.

The front door opens. I hear Mom move through the house, talking to herself, or to no one.

I lock my door, and sit in front of the habitat to collect my thoughts. My mother's footsteps move toward me down the hall, but they stop short of my room, and there's the sound of the bathroom door closing.

The shower runs. *Good.* I just want to stay here with the butterflies.

I watch the Jezebel scale the mesh, her colors flashing me as she moves to a perch and takes flight.

I did this.

I fixed her.

If only I could fix my mother so easily.

"Your mother will be fine. Let's buy butterflies!"

It's after one of our Sunday dinners that Nana suggests this. Mom has been acting weird all night. Not eating, staring off blankly in the middle of a thought. Slinking off to bed with talk of a migraine. Nana, per usual, is pretending everything is normal, head firmly planted in the sand.

I'd gone to the sink to help with the dishes, but she had shooed me away with a wave of her hand.

"I've got these," she'd said, sinking yellow-gloved hands into soapy water. "You go get your homework done so you don't end up like your boring old nana, cooking and cleaning without a thing of your own in the world."

Nana is wonderful—supportive and doting—but she can be infuriatingly old-fashioned and oblivious. Maybe because she never worked, and never had to, having married my pop-pop so young. He owned a shelving business that kept them comfortable, which she sold to a big closet company for a decent amount of money after he died. Kind of how Dad sold his vitamin company to the big conglomerate in California. But Nana acts like she had no options when she had plenty. After all, Aubrey's grandmother is an accountant at a fancy firm, and my friend Tanya's grandmother was my pediatrician in middle school. But I give

Nana leeway because with Dad still away, and Mom acting weird, she's the only adult I can count on.

In the living room I try to focus on my homework, but I'm distracted by thoughts about Mom, about Max Gordon, about Dad coming home, finally, he promises, in May. And, by the time Nana emerges from the kitchen, I'm perusing an online catalogue called *World of Butterflies*.

"Oh, my! Would you look at these!" Nana says, sitting next to me, clearly not annoyed that I'm procrastinating. "Are they real? What are they?"

"Yes, real," I say, clicking on the next close-up photo of a butterfly, transparent except for the wine-colored veins in its wings, as if it is made of stained glass. "Scientific name, *Greta oto*. More commonly known as a Glasswing."

I've been eyeing the Tropicals for months, ever since the second batch of Swallowtails and Monarchs I raised and set free in our yard last summer. The varieties are endless, so pretty they make me hyperventilate. At first, I thought I might try my hand at the Blue Morphos, but their life-span is short, and I can't bear the thought of them, all majestic like that, lying at the bottom of a habitat. So, instead, I've been looking at Glasswings, and a few others with longer lifespans.

"Glasswings, of course! That's exactly what they look like," Nana says, running her finger across the screen. I've told her a hundred times how it's bad for the computer, but I don't stop her. "They're quite stunning, aren't they? Shall we get some?"

"They're too expensive," I say. "They ship from the UK. And they don't even live here. It's too cold. They're tropical, indigenous to Chile, Mexico, and Panama. They've also been spotted in Texas. But not here. They don't belong here. There'd be no setting them free in our backyard. I'd need equipment. Lights. Plants. A way bigger habitat . . ."

"Don't you sound smart on all this," Nana says.

"I'm trying." I say. "I'm learning." And I am.

So far, I've only raised the common brushfoots and Swallowtails that came in the basic Butterfly House Kit Dad had given me before he left for LA, ones I'd set free the moment they emerged. These—the Tropicals—would be a lot more complicated.

"In that case, how about an early birthday present?" Nana asks, making me laugh. My birthday isn't until the end of June.

"Nana, that's months from now."

"Well, we'll have to get you something then, too. After all, a girl should have something truly special and beautiful when she turns sixteen."

I click to change the image on the screen, anything to distract Nana from talking about my birthday. Lately, she goes on and on about me becoming a woman, making me sure she's trying to hint something awkward about Max and me. She barely knows him, only that we're dating, and I haven't told her or Mom that he's a senior, or worse, that, since he was held back, he's already nineteen. Nana would have a stroke.

"Look at these," I say, stopping on a page full of Painted Jezebels. "These are my favorites," I tell her.

In the end, Nana chooses the Glasswings, *Greta oto,* and I choose the Painted Jezebels. *Delias hyparete metarete,* indigenous to Sri Lanka, India, and Southeast Asia.

The Glasswings are prettier, for sure. But I like the Jezebels with their plain white moth wings on top, their vibrant reds and oranges hidden underneath like a secret.

I watch the splinted Jezebel for a few minutes more to be sure she's really okay, before heading down the hall toward Mom's bedroom. I haven't heard a sound since she got out of the shower. But she's not in there; her bed is made up, no slight swell of the covers. Apparently she hasn't given up for the night yet.

A spark of hope flares in my chest. Maybe she's up doing something normal, cooking dinner in the kitchen for a change.

"Mom?" I call out. Maybe today with Dr. Marsdan was the magic session, and her therapy will have finally helped things. Maybe this new cocktail of medications is working.

At the entrance to the kitchen, hope deflates.

She sits with her back to me, in one of her dumb kimonos, her shoulders moving slightly, the sound of a pen scratching along an unseen sheet of paper.

She's writing one of those stupid letters. It would have been better if she were sleeping.

"Mom?" I have a hard time keeping the fear from my voice. "Mom."

She jerks her head around, her black tangle of hair whipping across her face. Her cheeks are wet. She's been crying. The sides of her short silk kimono—this one fuchsia with embroidered burgundy flowers trailing down the hem—fall open, revealing too much of her chest.

She looks at me, but doesn't see me.

I swallow hard and try again, louder, more forcefully. "Mom!

I told Nana she does this—disappears completely—and Nana says she asked Dr. Marsdan about it, and he said the trick is to re-ground her. "Give her facts that might pull her back to the present. She needs a little help focusing, that's all," Nana insisted.

Right, whatever.

"When did you get home?" I ask, trying. "Were you out shopping, or did you have an appointment with Dr. Marsdan?" Mom stares past me, eyes damp and distant. "Mom, was Nana with you?"

"What?" Her voice is soft, her question directed somewhere other than me.

"Mom. I'm asking you about today. Did Nana take you to your appointment with Dr. Marsdan, or did you go alone?"

With that, she snaps back, a mix of recognition and confusion playing across her face. "Oh, Jean Louise, yes. That's right. Nana, yes. She has her bridge group this evening. She went with me, but couldn't stay."

Okay, then.

Mom turns away again, sighs deeply, and folds the piece of paper on the table, jamming it into her pocket.

I look around our otherwise pristine kitchen, devoid of any cooking or baking or other culinary endeavor that might amount to a meal resembling dinner, and back at my mother. She's grown thinner these past weeks. The kimono hangs large at her shoulders.

Amidst the swirl of flowers is an embroidered symbol. It matches one my father sent me when he first moved out to

Malibu. It's the Japanese symbol for patience. I could use some of that right now.

"Mom?" I say, and she turns. "We should order something for dinner?"

"Yes. Yes. Of course we should. Could you call? Get me whatever you're having. I might need to rest for a bit." She heads to her room, leaving the pen, but taking the letter with her.

I think about calling Nana. At least last week Nana finally admitted that the doctor says Mom might have something seriously wrong with her. Something called dissociative disorder, which can cause both delusions and hallucinations. "It's only stress," Nana had added, reassuring herself, because she sure wasn't reassuring me. "Nothing to worry about, really. She'll be fine when your father gets home."

But what if she isn't?

And what if Dad never comes home?

Here's what I've learned, Aubrey: If a person is crazy but beautiful like my mother, they get away with it.

If they're rich and beautiful, even better.

Sure, maybe people talk behind their backs, hint and whisper, but mostly, they excuse it, or laugh it off. No one believes it. Or at least they don't see it for as serious as it is.

Take Lindsay Lohan or Shia LaBeouf, for example. Take Demi Lovato.

And, let's face it, my mother has always tended toward the dark and dramatic, the kind of person who has dancing-around-the-room highs, and crash-and-burn lows. Even when we were younger, you and I would say how weird she could act. Dad used to call it "free spirited."

"She's spontaneous!" you'd tell me. "Way better than my mom, who can't even sneeze on a whim." And, yeah, compared to your mother, with her crisp suits and white blouses, and endlessly booked schedule, my mother could be refreshing with her wild hair and bohemian clothes. She could be fun and exciting, but also mortifying, and not very parental, which, it turns out, only seems like a good thing, until it isn't.

But whatever you wanted to call it—her—before Dad left, after he left, she deteriorated.

No, worse than that, Aubrey. She unraveled. And not even Nana noticed how bad.

And somehow, you held that against _me_. As if I had any control over my mother . . .

I guess what I'm trying to say is, maybe if people saw beyond her beauty, they would have done more than gawk or roll their eyes when she whirled into the kitchen (or across the front lawn, or through the mall, or the bank, or the grocery store) laughing (or crying) in her hot-pink (or electric-blue, or mandarin-orange) kimonos which she had taken to wearing like street clothes. Heads turned, for sure, but nobody thought they should help her . . . Nobody thought they should try to help _me_.

God, even I loved those kimonos at first, remember, Aubrey? The matching turquoise ones Dad found in some little store on the beach in Malibu. "They were calling your names," he told us. "Real silk, for both of my butterflies."

He still calls me that, Aubrey, his butterfly.

If only I could ever feel like one.

"Wait, why do you have *that* on, Mom? It's freezing out. Seriously."

Mom drops her keys and handbag on the kitchen counter, and sits with her back to me, head in hands. She wears the turquoise kimono Dad sent, with flip-flops, which she apparently wore to take Dad to the airport early this morning, for his flight back to LA.

"I didn't get out of the car," she says, as if this makes it better.

It's nearly noon, and I'm groggy and upset that I overslept and she didn't wake me to say goodbye. At least he'll be home for good soon. He's been in LA for four months, so that means he only has two more to go. Six months gone altogether. "With one option period, two in a pinch. But not likely, so I wouldn't worry," he had reassured.

"Are you okay?" I ask her.

She turns to me, her eyes red and puffy from crying. "Should I be?"

"Mom, it's two more months, that's all. It will go fast. We'll be okay until he comes back." I'm trying to comfort her, even though it should be the other way around.

She shakes her head and puts it down on the table.

"Mom?" I watch her slim back rise and fall, swells of turquoise waves. "Mom, did something happen? Is everything okay?"

She shakes her head and gets up, walks to the cabinet, and rifles for some tea, ultimately tossing two open boxes to the floor, before slamming the cabinet shut. "Where the hell is the orange pekoe?"

"Mom?" She looks over at me.

"He's not coming home," she says.

"What? Why? Did he say that?"

"Six more months, apparently. Plus, the two remaining." She pulls a bottle of wine from the refrigerator, and practically slams a wineglass down on the counter. I wait for the shatter of glass. "They rented him his own fucking apartment in Malibu."

"Seriously? Why didn't he tell me last night?" Tears spring to my eyes. I fight them back because Mom can't handle me crying, too. She shrugs and uncorks the bottle. "It's barely noon, Mom," I say, but she glares at me, so I shut up. After another minute I ask, "It's okay, right? I mean, he's doing what he needs to do?"

She swallows down her wine and pours another. "It's only been four months," she says, "and I don't even recognize him anymore."

Remember when he came home for that visit, Aubrey? You were shocked by how different he looked, too. Only a few short months and already everything had changed. His ponytail gone, beard shaved, and every last tie-dyed T-shirt traded in for khaki pants, a polo shirt, and those god-awful sockless loafers.

But I kind of liked him better that way. It was as if he were suddenly a normal dad, one I could be proud of if he showed up at school. More like your parents. Like everyone elses.'

But my mother, she hated him for it. She wept and pummeled her fists against his chest like a child, begging him to come home and make everything the way it used to be. And now it would be eight more months instead of two.

I had called him that night, told him what a mess Mom was, asked him if there was anything he could do.

"Things change, Butterfly. The world changes," he had said. "We all need to change with it. Why don't you both come to LA? The schools are good. At least spend some time out here and see."

But I didn't want to go to school there. I had just started high school. We had. I didn't want to leave you. Not then.

After, I'd gone to my closet and dug out the dumb old starter habitat Dad had bought me four months before, left on my bed with a note taped to the box:

Jean Louise,
My favorite butterfly,
Something to distract you until I get home.
Love, Dad.

P.S. Send photos! Let me know how it goes.

I felt happy how he remembered my fourth-grade teacher had hatched Eastern Tiger Swallowtails in our classroom, how I had hatched them on my own after that. Our class had waited and watched for weeks, until finally, a dozen or so black-and-yellow-winged beauties emerged like fragile miracles. It was the week before Father's Day, so that Friday she'd invited all the dads to come in. We had cupcakes with butterflies on them, and released the Swallowtails out into the playground. All of them flew away except for one that took up residence on my shoulder. Dad and I stood there, amazed, as the butterfly just stayed and stayed there, its wings quivering, as if preparing to take flight, but changing its mind.

"Well, I guess it takes one to know one," Dad had said, delightedly taking photos of me to send Mom. That butterfly must have stayed on my shoulder for fifteen whole minutes before Katy Meisler got jealous and tried to cup it in her hands, chasing it away.

I raised that first round last spring, and a second later that summer, each cycle marking time, like that first quivering Swallowtail on my shoulder, until my father would come back home to us.

But, of course, both rounds of common butterflies had come and gone, and even the Tropicals had hatched without seeing his return.

It took me coming here, to finally bring him home.

Now, he says we'll go home together and face Mom.

But here's the thing, Aubrey: he doesn't know what I'm about to tell you.

And, those letters? They were only the beginning of it all.

When Mom goes to sleep, I watch the butterflies, the splinted Jezebel I still can't believe I helped. When it's late enough that Dad might be home, I move to the living room couch in the soundless blue glow of the television, my homework untouched, and dial him again, missing the days when I was excited to talk to him, when every conversation wasn't laden with an overwhelming dread.

It rings five times before he picks up. I was kind of hoping he wouldn't; I have a bad sinking feeling in my gut.

"Hey, Butterfly." He sounds winded, distracted. "Let me turn down the music. I'm on the treadmill." Joe Cocker, or some other guy with a Joe Cocker–like gravelly voice, blares, then quiets in the background. "Oh shit! Be right there. I forgot I had something on the stove."

The phone muffles, then clanks down, and I hear Dad curse some more in the background. At least he must be alone, so that's a good thing.

My eyes shift to the coffee table, to the large glossy book, *The Beat Generation,* with Jack Kerouac's face plastered all over the black-and-white cover. Repeating images of him in different squares, collaged around a larger one in the center. There's one in the top right corner that if you added a little scruff to it, I swear would look just like Max.

I stretch my leg, using my bare toes to shove the book to the corner, then off the table, altogether. It lands on the rug with a satisfying thud.

I hate that dumb book. The letter writing started right after Nana gave it to Mom, and told us all her old stories again. She and Nana are always going on about the guy, some long-dead author who no one cares about anymore. Just because Nana met him once when she was young.

The Kerouac letters weren't the only sign of my mother being crazy, though. There was the constant crying, the sleeping, the heavy drinking, and recently the talking to herself or, more accurately, the conversations she started having with my dad when he wasn't there. Calling him by name, laughing with him all flirty and weird, when it was clear they weren't on the phone.

I'd walk past her bedroom and hear her talking to him, but when I peeked in, there was no phone in sight, no laptop open. Only Mom, alone, sitting on the edge of her bed staring at the wall.

"JL? You there? I'm really sorry, hon. Did you hear what I said?"

Dad's voice drifts back to me. When did he pick up again? And why is he apologizing?

"No." The word sticks in my throat. I want to hang up. I shouldn't have called. He barely checks in anymore. Not really. Not unless he has bad news.

"They extended the contract, sweetheart . . . nothing I could help. They have the right . . . two options . . . practically begged me . . . end of August, latest . . . swear . . . come out . . . stay the summer here."

The room reels. I don't want to hear the rest of his words.

Instead, I count on my fingers. It's the same deal as last time. "But that's four more months, Dad, and Mom isn't doing so well." I stop, swallow back more tears. Telling him will only make him want to stay away longer.

"I know, honey. I feel awful. This is the absolute last extension I have to honor."

But I'm not listening anymore. I'm lost in the collage of Kerouac's face, staring up at me through the glass square of the coffee table.

I drop the stack of bills and Mom's letter in the box, right as Benny drives up, my favorite mailman. He's been delivering our mail since I was little.

"I've got those!" he calls from the curb, his hand stretched out the open mail truck door. I walk over, smiling, and place them in his hand. He quickly sorts through them and frowns.

"You sure about this one?" He hands it back to me, the letter Mom gave me to mail, a sympathetic look on his face. "The addressee," he says.

I read the name, my brain only partially registering:

Mr. Jean-Louis Kerouac
7 Judy Ann Court
Northport, NY 11768

I blink, confused, not only by Kerouac's last name, but also by the familiar letters of my own first name—Jean Louise—preceding it. When I manage to look up, Benny says, "It's not the first one. All last month. They kept on coming. Letter after letter to the same address."

He disappears below the window like he's retrieving something from under his seat, and reappears with a rubber-banded bundle of envelopes, all stamped *Return to Sender*.

"It would be a federal offense for me not to mail them, but once they come back . . . Well, I was hoping to maybe catch your mother in person."

I take the stack reluctantly, and thumb through them.

"Wait," I finally say. "Are these all to him? *Jack* Kerouac?"

Benny shrugs. "I wasn't sure at first myself. Never read the guy so I didn't realize from the name, had only ever heard of him referred to as Jack. But the address . . . well, most of us older folks, we know the famous addresses along our routes, you know? They ring a bell. So I asked around . . ."

I nod, wondering how many people at the post office now know my mother is insane.

"My route sub, Shauna, she grew up nearby, and recognized the address immediately." He nods at my hand clutching the letters. "Turns out anyone from around here knows Kerouac lived over there. Same as we know Billy Joel comes from Hicksville, or Alec Baldwin hails from the South Shore. You know how it is."

I nod again, even though I don't know. I don't know anything except that I'm holding some messed-up letters from my mother.

"Yeah," I say, forcing my gaze up to Benny's. "Thanks for this. These. Thanks for not telling anyone."

"Hey," he says, trying to turn his voice hopeful. "Maybe that's not who she meant to send them to? Maybe they're meant for some sort of relative? But, rest assured, there is no one at that address by that name. Not anymore. I could talk to her. But maybe it's better if you do."

"Yeah, better from me," I say. "Thank you."

After he leaves, I sit on the stoop, my heart sinking, and tear open the first envelope, the one she was mailing today. Maybe there's a logical explanation. Maybe Nana knew him better than she let on. Maybe Jack Kerouac is really my grandfather! Maybe there's some dark family secret I'm not aware of.

But if that were true, Nana would have told me. She wouldn't have kept it from me so many years after Pop-pop died.

I unfold the letter, and force myself to read.

After a few brief lines, it becomes more than clear.

He wasn't my grandfather.

It isn't about Nana.

My mother is writing love letters to a dead man.

Max lies under me, one arm folded behind his head like a pillow, my long brown hair falling over us like a curtain, shielding us from the world. I wanted him to come see the Jezebel. A few days later and you can barely tell the splint from her wing.

I lean down and kiss his eyelids and he smiles. We've been dating nearly two whole months already.

I think this, but don't mention it. We're already taking things way slower than he wants. No need to point out how long. Everyone knows Max isn't a virgin, but I'm hoping to hold out until I turn sixteen. Sixteen seems reasonable. I know other girls who have lost their virginity at sixteen. So, it can't be that slutty or Jezebel-like, not that I give a crap what Aubrey thinks. Even Nana says sixteen is when a girl becomes a woman.

And, not that Max is complaining. Not directly. Not yet. But I can tell he's losing patience.

"Mmmm," he says, grabbing my ass and pulling me tighter against him, as if reading my thoughts. He kisses me hard and shakes his head. "God, you're—" He stops, and motors his lips, his whole body shuddering, like a dog shaking off freezing water. He reaches down, under me, and adjusts himself through his jeans. "Breaking me," he finishes. "You're absolutely fucking killing me, Jailbait."

So maybe he is complaining.

"I am?" I shift my weight off him, concerned, but he pulls me back against him, so that even through his jeans I can feel him there, hard and pulsing beneath my pelvic bone.

"No, it's fine. Stay. It's just . . . See what you do to me? Think you'd be willing to finish me off?"

"Like—?"

"Hand. Mouth. Dealer's choice. Just so you don't leave me hanging here like this."

"Oh," I say, my face flushing warm.

"Never mind," he says fast. "It's okay. You stay here, and I'll do it." He closes his eyes and slides me up and down against him, up and down. I close mine, too, lost in the motion until I'm aching, feeling like I might be on the verge. If only I didn't need to wait. "Is this all right?" he whispers.

"Yes," I say, "yes," and I mean it. After all, we have our clothes on, and I like the way it feels, Max hard against me, urgent and wanting me so bad. I'm lost in the rhythm, trying to imagine what it would be like if we did it right this second. It sends a thrill through me. *What if I actually am ready?*

"I want you, too," I whisper back. "I swear I do. I just need a little more time."

"Uh-huh."

"Max, I do. Really."

"Shhh, it's all good." He moves me faster, and one of his hands slips down my skirt, down the back of my underpants. I let him keep it there, trying not to think too hard about any of it. But what if my mother comes home?

"Don't stop me, okay?" Max moans and grunts a little,

which makes my stomach swirl, so there's no way I'd even dare.

Instead, I lower my mouth over his, and let our tongues mix, and lose myself in the motion, until he shakes hard once, then again, like a series of little earthquakes are moving through him.

"Oh man, shit, sorry," he says, sitting up. "I'll be right back," and he jumps up and disappears into the hall.

The bathroom door closes.

I stare at the ceiling, and smile. I did that for him. *With* him.

When he returns, he lies back down and rolls toward me. "You're beautiful, you know that?" he says.

My heart soars. "And what else?"

"What do you mean?"

"Earlier, you said I am something. Besides killing you, that is."

He thinks for a second. "Besides killing me, is there anything good left to be?" He smiles his big, cheesy smile, but I shake my head like that's not good enough, so he says, "Okay, how about this? You're a 'bud of love,' Jailbait. 'By summer's ripening breath.' 'A bud of love.'"

"Huh," I say, satisfied, even if I have only the faintest idea what he's talking about. He's quoting something. A sonnet. A poem. Robert Frost or Emily Dickinson, or someone.

"Shakespeare," he says, not waiting for me to guess and get it wrong.

I lay my cheek on his chest, and listen to his heartbeat. "Tell me more."

He strokes the side of my cheek with his thumb. "Okay, fine. How fares thee, my JL? 'That I ask again; For nothing can be ill, if she be well.'"

I smile, my cheek warm under the touch of his thumb. "What's that from?"

"Guess."

"*Romeo and Juliet?*"

He nods. "Very good! Butchered pretty bad, but still. Jesus, don't you kids read at all anymore?"

I kick him playfully, and roll away from him, onto my back. "I read," I say. "Plenty. Just not Shakespeare. Yuck. Can't understand a word of his."

"Really?"

"Really," I say. "Who even needs to?"

"Everyone, Jailbait. Do you know how many modern musicians sample Shakespeare or retell his stories in song? The Beatles. Radiohead. Iron Maiden. Metallica."

"Who?"

He shakes his head. "Okay, here's one more your speed: Taylor Swift."

"Does not."

"Does too. 'Love Story.' Total rip-off of Romeo and Juliet. And I think a few others of hers, though I'm not really a Taylor Swift fan."

"Oh, you're right," I say. "I remember the video now. You sure do know a lot about Taylor Swift for a biker dude."

He laughs, and rests his hand on my head, his fingers tangling with my hair. On the ceiling above us, there's an X-shaped crack. I reach up and follow it with my finger as I've done a hundred times before, this time taking it as a sign: *X marks the spot* where I'm here with Max Gordon. Just like I'm supposed to be.

"How do you know all those poems you quote?" I ask. "The plays. All the stuff in Hankins' lit class?"

He shrugs. "Not all of it. Barely anything, really. But I will one day. I'm on a quest to read it all."

"You are?"

He untangles his fingers, rolls onto his back, and pulls

me decisively on top of him. I must look concerned, because he says, "Don't worry, I just want to talk to you. Not do anything. But, yeah, Jailbait, I'm on a lot of quests, and, I won't lie, you're one of them. But in a good way. I like you. A lot. So, I want to touch you. I want to feel you. And, yes, I want to sleep with you—make love to you." He makes a face at his words. "I want to be inside of you because I want to know every inch of you there is to know." My stomach lurches, but he quickly adds, "Don't worry. I don't mean now, this second. But I'm a big boy, and you're a big girl, right? And the things I want to do with you, they're natural. They're fun. I promise you that. And, it's just skin. Fingers. Body parts. I want mine on you. *In* you. I want to make you feel good."

His words take my breath away, make my cheeks burn, my heart race, and my insides melt and float away.

"I want that, too, Max," I say, but who knows if he hears me. That last part is barely even sound.

About the whole "Jailbait" thing, Aubrey, let's get that out of the way.

I know you thought it was crude, but he was only being funny, teasing because I was younger than him. A simple play on words.

It started because he was singing this song called "Jolene" that apparently Miley Cyrus sings. Except it's not her song, but someone else's, and really old. Anyway, at first he was singing it the right way, and then, instead of singing her name—Jolene—he started to sing mine, JL. "JL, JL, Jay-ay El, jay-ell"—like that, with a country twang, and he realized it sounded like "jail."

"Hey, that's what you are," he had said, winking. "Jailbait. Since you keep reminding me how young and innocent you are."

"I'm not reminding you," I'd said. But, of course, I constantly did.

And you know the funny thing, Aubrey? Regardless of what you and those girls thought of me, Max was right. For as much as you and I fantasized about things in the safety of our bedrooms—your bedroom—in the end, I was way too innocent for my own good.

SUMMER
BEFORE SIXTH GRADE

"Wait, what are you doing, Aubs?" I ask. You've gotten up from your bed where we were just kissing pillows and playing pretend, to shut your bedroom door.

We're alone. Your parents are at work, having decided we are finally old enough to be left here on our own during the day. But Ethan will be home from tennis camp any minute. "I don't want him spying on us," you say, rolling your eyes.

We're playing Boyfriends, which used to be called House or Dress Up, but it's taken more of a grown-up turn, so we don't call it those other things anymore. It's been months since we've bothered with the old trunk of clothes in your basement, where we used to fish out your mother's dresses and pretend to go off to fake jobs, or fake restaurants and Broadway shows.

"Shhh, hold on. I have to show you something," you say, turning the lock. "I got the idea from a video on YouTube."

I watch you with the same suspicious look you watched me with last week, when I first suggested we practice kissing our invisible boyfriends for real. "Trust me, it works," I had told you. "It makes you tingle in all sorts of places." We'd spent countless hours since placing our open lips to the backs of our hands, moving our tongues in circles over the surface of our own soft skin. Then last week, we had advanced to using pillows as their bodies.

You cross to your desk where you moved Mary Lennox, so we had room to spread out on the top of your lacy bedspread.

"What are you doing with her?" I ask.

"You'll see. Promise me you won't get all weird."

I had bought Mary Lennox for you last year at a garage sale, a present for your eleventh birthday, even though you were already too old for her. She was a vintage doll, still in her box, sealed up like new with a flowered dress, shiny black shoes, and dark curly hair.

You had gone nuts for her, like I knew you would. You still collected dolls back then. Naming her Mary Lennox after the character in *The Secret Garden,* you gave her the most prime real estate at the head of your bed.

Now, you carry her over and place her on top of your bed, lying down. Your face is serious, concentrating, as you lift up her dress to reveal bland white panties and a bare flat chest underneath.

"Promise you won't tell," you whisper, but it's not a question; you know I am safe, that I am the person you can trust. "I call her Martin Leonard," you say. "Only for this. And I take her dress up, so she feels like more of a boy."

You crawl on top of her, position your body down over hers, your mouth on hers, and start kissing. After a minute, it's like you forget I'm there and you let out these soft little moaning noises. Right there in front of me, you're humping a life-sized doll.

I've never been more desperate to try anything.

When you finally stop, your cheeks are pink and warm. You get up.

"You want to try now?" you ask me.

"Okay," I say.

I crawl onto her, my heart pounding, and press my lips to hers, disappointed at their hard plastic that has no give. Still, within minutes, I'm flushed and lost in it all, moving shamelessly against her like you were.

When I'm done, you put Mary Lennox back on your desk and lie down next to me, and we breathe side by side.

"Promise me you won't ever tell. Not a word about Martin Leonard."

"Okay, I won't," I say, relieved you didn't hear me call her Ethan out loud.

"Can we let them out?" Max asks. Mom has an appointment with Dr. Marsdan today, so I invited him over after school. We haven't been together much since last week.

"Yeah." I close my bedroom door, and wrap my arms around his shoulders and kiss the back of his head, my lips lingering in his tousled hair.

In the habitat, the Jezebel with the wing I fixed crawls up the mesh side closest to us.

"There she is," I say, pointing. "The one I fixed." I move my finger along where she walks, my heart swelling. "She's still hanging in. I can't believe it."

"How do you know it's a she?" Max asks.

"I can't swear it," I say, "but I think so. The black veins on the females' wings are thicker."

"Uh-huh," Max says, and I punch his arm playfully.

"You were hoping for something more anatomical?" He turns to me, sincerity registering on his scruffy face.

"Don't worry about the sex stuff, Jailbait. Really. I mean it. I told you, I'm not like that. I swear. And anyway, I'm on hiatus, if you must know. What did that weird actor do, re-member?" I shrug, clueless. "Oh yeah, his chi. Something to do with his chi. I'm doing that. Recharging my chi, or regaining it, I forget which. But by the time you're ready, it'll be like I'm a virgin all over again."

I roll my eyes, but he takes my hand and pulls me down next to him. "I'm serious, Jailbait. I like you. I'm not just in it to fuck your brains out, no matter what you've heard about me. I like the other stuff, too. All the kissing and shit. Talking to you. How you like all this butterfly crap." He nods at the habitat.

"Well, when you put it that way," I say, and he laughs.

"No, but I mean it. You care about stuff other people wouldn't. You make me feel like I can tell you stuff, like you care that I'm here."

It's not what I'm expecting, and it makes me feel uncomfortable and I don't even know why. I feel responsible for him, suddenly. Because I get what he's saying.

Even he wants to belong somewhere.

SUMMER
AFTER SIXTH GRADE

It's the weekend before middle school starts, and several of our friends have been set free for the night, off to the YMCA carnival without parents, roaming in cliques, their pockets stuffed with tickets, no one telling them how much fried dough not to eat, or what ride not to go on.

I'm allowed to go parentless, but you're not, so you say it should be my parents who supervise us because they are cooler, but I argue it should be yours. I want a fresh start in middle school. I don't want to be known forever as the girl with the weirdo hippy parents, my mother coming to class parties in her floppy hats and long, flowing tie-dye skirts, and my dad in his goofy sandals, talking about herbal vitamins, his ponytail practically down to his butt. And unlike you, I have no Ethan, no drop-dead-gorgeous, star older brother, to buffer or pave the way.

"How about Ethan?" I blurt, the idea popping into my head. "He's starting high school, so he's practically a grown-up, right? What if your parents let him take us instead?"

"I'll ask," you say. "But I doubt it."

They do, though, making him promise not to take his eyes off us the entire time, and making us promise not to make him chase after us.

It's the other way around. Ethan spots a bunch of his

friends walking in and takes off the minute your parents are gone, calling after us to meet him back at the ticket booth, "Right in this spot, exactly two hours from now."

"Aye, aye, Captain," we chime back together, doing our best impression of the *SpongeBob* opening. You elbow me and give me a "well-we-pulled-this-off" look, and we're off on our own at the YMCA carnival.

It's a perfect late summer evening, the melancholy of the too-soon chill in the August air immediately erased by the cheerful twang of piped-in calliope music and the dizzying blur of the Technicolor lights. We're giddy as we run off to scope out food and rides.

On the line for the Tilt-A-Whirl, you lean in and whisper, "Don't be obvious, but, ew, gross, look over there." I've pulled a chunk of rainbow cotton candy from the stick and hand it over to you.

"Where?"

"Don't be obvious," you repeat. "By the bathrooms, there."

I twist around slowly, trying to be nonchalant, but don't see anything.

"What, Aubrey?"

You pull off a smaller piece of spun sugar and place it on your tongue, sticking it out so I can watch the pastel colors deepen as they melt away. "Not a what, a who," you say, when it's gone. "Those two, making out in the corner."

"Oh." I can't make out their faces, because they're glued together at the mouth. "So what?" I ask because aren't I desperate for the day when I can make out with a guy by a bathroom stall or anywhere? And I thought you felt the same. We're always talking about it, imagining it. Choosing from boys in our class. Pretending on dolls.

"Nothing. It's just, that's Janee Freese. With Rebecca Goldberg's brother."

"So?" Janee Freese is our friend Tanya's sister, although we're way better friends with Tanya, and Rebecca Goldberg is one of our newer friends we met through Tanya, because they went to camp together.

"Geez, JL, don't you know the rules at all? Brothers are off-limits. Even across grades."

"They are? How come?" You give me a look like I'm dumb. "Okay, got it," I say, looking back at Janee with envy. But I don't. Not completely. "But what if Rebecca doesn't care?"

"Trust me, she'll care."

"Are you going to tell her?"

"Of course I'm going to tell her. That's what friends do."

Is it? I wonder.

I nod anyway, and try to work up a dislike for Janee the way you have. But I can't seem to. So what if they're kissing? It's not like they're stealing, or doing something wrong.

All through the Tilt-A-Whirl and Pirate Ship, I'm distracted and mad and sad. I want someone to kiss me one day the way Rebecca's brother is kissing Janee. I want to tell you to mind your own business, to not start trouble where there is none. To leave Janee and What's His Name alone. *Is this what middle school is going to be full of?*

After the Pirate Ship, I feel sick. I think about calling Dad to pick me up and take me home, but you grab my hand—me practically wincing at your touch—and say, "Shoot, JL, it's past nine! Ethan is going to kill us!" and we break into a run. When we reach the ticket booth, he's not even there, and you yell dramatically at the top of your lungs in some weird, unidentifiable accent, "The lying bastard!" and I bust out laughing at that, because I can't even help myself, and just like that, everything is good between us again.

And, when we do find him, over by the goldfish game—the one where you have to toss quarters into the bowls—he's holding court there, surrounded by a group of friends, mostly girls, clutching neon-colored stuffed animals, all fawning over him, his golden-haired self in the center, shining in the artificial lights. And all I can think about is what it must be like to be you, to be Ethan, to be either one of you super-perfect Anderssons.

But I don't have to wonder because you grab my hand and pull me into the center of that circle, and say, "This is my sister, guys. Jean Louise. But everyone calls her JL."

And everyone crowds around me, now, too, so in that moment, like so many moments with you, I can feel perfect, too.

I let go of Max's hand, and open the Velcro closure of the habitat, folding the mesh panel back and pressing it onto its hooks.

"These, over here?" I say. "The Jezebels? Predators can't eat them because of their toxins. Their bright colors tell you that. Even before they hatch, you can tell from the neon yellow of their chrysalis."

"Cool," Max says. "And these?"

"Glasswings are the opposite, which makes them more susceptible. But they can store temporary toxins from the plants they eat. Plus, their transparency protects them."

"Opposite of humans," Max says.

I'm about to point out more nerdy butterfly facts, or try to urge a few of the butterflies out of the habitat, but I notice two Glasswings coupled and going at it unceremoniously in the corner. They look like one butterfly with eight wings.

Max notices, too.

"Get a room, huh?" he says, laughing. He sits back, watching them for a minute; then, as if they've given him the idea, he wraps his arms around me, and pulls me down, lowering me onto my carpet. He breathes into my hair like he's trying to inhale me. "We could do like them, if you want to."

"Max . . ." I whisper in warning, though to him or me lately I'm never really sure. "What happened to your chi thing?"

"I changed my mind," he says. "Just a little more?"

"Okay, but just a little." And then his tongue is meeting mine, and his hands are under my shirt, then under my bra, his fingers finding my nipples, sending my thoughts spinning, and me and this room careening into outer space.

LATE APRIL
TENTH GRADE

The front door closes, and my eyes snap open, confused.

The light has grown dim, slipping in weakly through the translucent shades of my window. We've fallen asleep on the floor, limbs wrapped together, my head on Max's chest. I untangle myself, and sit up, pulling my T-shirt back down. I'm still fully clothed, but Mom would kill me. Or Nana, if she happens to be here. Or Mom might call Dad, but if he wants to parent me, he's just going to have to come home.

"Max, get up." I go to shake him, but his eyes are wide open.

"I am up, goofball. That's why you're up. I was talking to you."

"You were? I think my mom came home. How long was I asleep?" Max rolls on his side, props up on an elbow, and looks at me. He seems like he's been awake for a while.

Was he watching me the whole time?

"Not long." He shrugs. "And, yeah, someone came in."

"What were you doing?"

"Nothing. Resting. Thinking."

"About what?" I search for my cell phone—My bed? My desk?—I can't seem to gauge what time it is.

"California."

"Wait, what? How come?" I ask, retrieving it from my night table. It's already 6:20. I have no texts or messages from Mom. I feel groggy, drugged. When I move back toward Max, I realize the cotton of my underwear is damp.

"Because I'm going. And I needed to tell you."

"You are?" Panic rises in my chest.

"Yes."

"When?" Tears form because I'm so tired and out of it, I don't have the chance to brace myself.

"Soon as I graduate. You should come."

I sit on the edge of my bed, and try to collect myself, and bring my room into crisp focus. Desk. Closet. Butterfly habitat. In the distance, the sound of water running. Another door opening and closing. The pad of my mother's feet—only hers, no other footsteps, no conversation—moving through the house.

Will she come down the hall and check on me?

Does she even know I exist?

"But why?"

"Because I want to. Because I can. Because I hate it here and there's nothing here for me, other than you." My eyes dart to him. Did I know this? Did I have any clue Max was unhappy? "Because it's always warm there. No winter. No sleet. No snow."

"But—"

"But nothing, Jailbait. I'm going. So, come with me. Please. I want you to. I bet they have all sorts of butterflies there."

"Come on over here, JL. You can sit next to me," Ethan calls to me as soon as I reach the bottom of the stairs. He pats the seat of the big orange armchair where he's already sitting, a grease-smeared paper plate in his lap. His sneakered feet are up on the ottoman, where I could, otherwise, sit.

My heart skips a beat. The rest of the couch and chairs are taken, but he could move his feet and I wouldn't have to be there, squished right next to him.

I should tell him to move them. I should *choose* not to sit that close to him.

It's a Saturday, late afternoon, and I've walked here, as usual, despite the storm outside. The skies opened up right as I reached your front door. My hair is wet and the basement air is cold on my damp skin. Goose bumps rise up and I shiver.

I could go upstairs and get a towel. You're up there, still showering. You came home from the soccer fields covered in mud.

Party at my house, you had texted. If you get there first, save me a slice. E won't.

Now the rich, sweet and sour smell of dough and sauce and garlic hit my nose, and remind me, so I veer toward the bar instead. This is willpower, since my window of opportunity is limited. Anyway, I'm not comfortable wading past all of Ethan's friends to get to him.

Behind the bar, I slide two slices out of the open box and onto plates, and set those off to the side.

"Hurry up, Markham!" your brother calls, twisting to look where I've gone. "Oh!" he says, realizing. "While you're there, bring me another one." He holds up his empty plate, and I slide a third slice onto a fresh one, my eyes shifting to the stairs because, for a second, I think I hear you coming. But now I have a legitimate reason. I'm just delivering his food because he asked me to.

I make my way across the room, my heart beating so hard it's ridiculous. I can't help it, and, trust me, I want to. This has been going on for months, this thing where I can't wait to see Ethan, where I read into everything, hoping. Even when I know there's no way he's interested.

Except, I feel like he is. I've noticed him watching me lately, calling me over when I walk in a room. Being over-friendly and squeezing my shoulders, or bumping my arm. Last week, he offered me a ride home, when I've been walking to and from your house alone for the past four years.

"I'll take you; it's raining," he said, though it was barely sprinkling. *He just got his license,* I told myself. *He wants an excuse to drive.*

"Markham," he demands, making me realize I've stopped halfway there. "Quick, you have to see this, before he's done."

I nod, my cheeks burning as I weave through his friends who have spilled off the couch and onto the floor. A girl I recognize from chorus is perched on the lap of a boy from tennis team.

I move to the orange chair where Ethan is and hand his plate to him.

"Here." He pats the arm of the chair.

There's nowhere else. That's all.

I sit, and he takes a bite of pizza, propping the plate on his legs. Our arms are practically touching. "Watch this," he says mouth full, and nods to the television where a Ninja Warrior episode or something is blasting. "It's unbelievable. Dude has one leg."

On the screen, a good-looking black man is making his way across obstacles in camouflage pants, no shirt, and ripped six-pack abs. Like Ethan said, he's on only one leg. Still, I have to fight to pay attention. I can feel my arm hairs stand when they brush against his.

"It's amazing," I finally twist to tell him. But, when I do, he's already looking at me, our faces too close, his expression an intense question that makes it hard for me to breathe.

The room erupts with a collective gasp as the guy falls from an obstacle into the water.

"That was freaking crazy!" the girl sitting on the arm of the couch says. "I don't care that he didn't finish. They should still give him the money or trophy, or whatever." She gets up and walks over to where we are and lifts Ethan's plate, collapsing down backward onto his lap. "What do you think, Ethan? Finish or not, don't you think he should get the money?"

She reaches her arm up and wraps it behind Ethan's neck, as if I'm not here, as if I'm a no-one, as if I don't matter, which I don't. I feel like I'm going to puke.

I unwedge myself, and get up, and walk back to the bar, but I'm really not hungry anymore, and a few minutes later, you're downstairs, and someone turns on the movie, and we eat room temp pizza together while I try my hardest not to think about how awful I am, or, worse, make one single wish I'm not supposed to have.

SPRING
SEVENTH GRADE

1. *Always be friends.*
2. ~~*Never fight.*~~ *If we fight, always make up.*
3. *Never date a boy the other person likes. Siblings included, because Janee Freese is gross.*
4. *Never leave the other person alone in the cafeteria.*
5. *Always keep each other's secrets no matter what.*
6. *Never keep secrets from each other.*

You hand the pen to me, but I shake my head.

"I'm sure you thought of everything," I say.

"Come back here, Jailbait. Don't be upset."

Max has moved to my bed, but I move to the habitat and watch the butterflies.

How is he only telling me about California now, with less than six weeks left of school?

Is this how much I matter to him?

Why didn't he tell me in February, when we first started dating, when I had time to protect myself, or at least earlier today—or yesterday—when we had all the time in the world? Now my mother is home and all I want to do is get him out of here.

"You have to go, Max," I say, trying not to sound mad or, worse, let the tears that want to come, fall. "I have a ton of homework."

"Jailbait—"

"Max, please." The tears break through and, for a second, I can barely hold on to myself. He gets up and walks over, and wraps his arms tightly around me, burying his face in my neck.

I shake him off. I'm not doing this. But he holds on tighter.

"I care about you. A lot. I swear."

"Max, don't." I squirm free from his hug and swipe at

my eyes. I'm dumb for crying, and even more dumb for being so needy and naïve. What did I think was going to happen once he graduated? Did I think he'd hang around for some babyish, virgin sixteen-year-old?

I stand there feeling stupid and alone. I want to put on dry underpants, erase all reminders of him touching me.

No. I want the opposite: I want him to touch me more, to do everything with me, and promise me he'll never leave.

"Can we talk about this, please?" he finally asks.

I crouch down, and reach in to move an orange slice from one perch to another, needing to be busy doing something, to not look at Max. He had asked to take them out earlier, but I don't feel like letting them out anymore. I want them to stay safe as long as they can, tucked inside the mesh screen.

I close the Velcro flap again, and a Glasswing crawls up the side. I touch its foot through the mesh thinking it will fly away, but it stays there, looking at me.

"In Costa Rica," I say, my voice wobbly, "they call Glasswings *Espejitos*. Spanish for 'little mirrors.'"

I squint my eyes and stare at its wings, hoping I might see myself there. But I don't. I can't. They don't reflect anything. Even those words are a lie. I'm nowhere to be found these days.

But that's not true, is it? Max cares about me. That's what he said.

"I want you, Jailbait." How many times has he told me that? Isn't that kind of the same as love?

I should stop stalling, and have sex with him. Run off to California just like Dad did.

"JL?"

"Yeah?"

"It's okay."

In the hallway, a door opens and closes, and the sound

of the television drifts to me. At least Mom is leaving me alone.

I turn and look up at him, and he comes over to sit next to me, and rubs away a tear that's slipped down my cheek.

"No need to be sad," he says. "We still have time. I have plenty of plans to work out. I bought this bike, did I tell you? Not a dirt bike. The real deal. I want you to see her, feel her, but she's not road-ready yet. She needs parts. A better engine. I blew all my savings on her, and paying some of Dad's bills. I've got to make more money before I can fix her up and go." He tips my chin, and looks deep into my eyes. "I really want you to come with me."

And like that, I'm hit with a new emotion: Excitement. Maybe even hope. I could do it. Leave here and go to California with Max. I'm not sure exactly how, but Dad is still there, so if I wanted to, I could! I could make up some lies, leave out some facts, and go.

Go *with* him. Even help him to go.

With this thought, a memory, stuck to an idea, darts at the edges of my brain: Mom and Dad, dancing. Celebrating.

And something else.

It hasn't quite surfaced yet.

And it shouldn't.

It shouldn't.

But another drop of anger and it will.

FALL
NINTH GRADE

"We're goddamned rich, Charlotte; can you believe it? No more late fees and ridiculous interest. We can pay it all off! The credit cards, the leases. Hell, the mortgage! No more money worries, ever again!" He picks her up and spins, but she holds herself stiff.

"Put me down, Tom."

Dad, still in his rented tuxedo, obliges, but holds her hand, and tries to twirl her out in front of him in her lacy black dress.

"Look how beautiful you are! Beautiful and rich!"

"I said stop."

He pulls her tight to his chest and kisses the top of her head. "You worry too much. It will all be fine. After this, I never even have to work again."

"I don't care." She turns away from him in her bare feet, revealing the unzipped back of the dress. He puts a hand on her shoulder, and she whirls around, angry, her face wet with tears.

"You were okay with this, Char . . . ?" he says, but it's more like a question. "All of this. We talked about it. And all night you were fine." He tips her face up. "Drinking champagne, dancing, celebrating. Those assholes from LA couldn't take their eyes off of you. You know it's going to be okay. . . ."

She slaps his hand away, and yanks down her dress, stands there in only her black bra and lacy underwear. I want to back away from the crack in their half-open door, where I've been watching, listening, but I'm afraid to make a noise.

"I lied! I faked it!" my mother yells. "You know I'm an excellent faker. I don't want this. Not if it's going to be that long. Six months! Half a year! I want you. Us. To all stay here. Together."

"Charlotte, six months is nothing. The time will fly. We're talking seven figures and a cash bonus . . ."

When he tries to grab hold of her arm, she wheels away. "I'm going to bed," she says, and the door to her bathroom slams.

"Char. Come on, Char . . . ?" Dad follows, disappearing from my view. A few minutes later, they return, my father still trailing behind.

Not five hours earlier, they had headed off to a celebratory dinner and contract signing at the Rainbow Room in New York City, with the guys who were buying Dad's company. Mom had gotten all dressed up in her new dress and heels, and Dad had apparently rented a tuxedo. They looked like movie stars. My parents never looked like that, all dressed up and glamorous. They looked happy.

And fifteen minutes ago, they'd come back, laughing and giddy.

I had come out of my room to witness that—the glee and excitement—but by the time I reached their bedroom door, everything had shifted.

Now my mother lies facedown, still in her undergarments, on the bed. My father sits beside her. He reaches a hand out to touch her back but thinks better of it, and rests it in his lap.

My mother is prone to these fits more and more lately—her tantrums. She shouldn't be mad at him. Not if it's going to make everything easier. I'm sure he doesn't want to go. And I don't want him to go, either.

But she should make it easier for him. Get over it. It's not like she's ever had to work.

After a few minutes, he reaches out and strokes her back, and she lets him. "I'll be home soon," he says, softly. "You'll see. You're being dramatic. You won't even miss me."

"I will." She flips over and sits up, puts her head in her hands. When she takes them away she says, "And you told them you could stay longer . . ."

"I didn't tell them that. It's an option, a contract thing. It's the only way their lawyer would let them make the deal. I'm a 'key man,' Char. I have to make sure they're up and running. Introduce them to vendors, buyers, how to do the studies, schmooze the customers. You know how it goes."

"Bullshit," she says. "You want to go, or you wouldn't."

"Stop it, Charlotte. I'm serious. For once in your life be practical." He gets up, and walks over to the chair in the corner, and retrieves a briefcase that he places on the bed. He snaps the locks and yanks the top open. *"This,"* he says, "is practical." He tips the briefcase over and wrapped piles of bills fall onto the bedspread. "Cash. And, there's plenty. Whatever you and JL need . . . Whatever we need. Even your goddamned mother . . . Buy her a car. And that's only one installment. There's more where that came from."

She stares at the wads of green paper.

"They paid you cash?"

"Just a small bonus. Charlotte, this is nothing. . . ."

"I don't care," she says, shoving a few of the stacks aside. "I don't want it." Her voice is small, petulant like a child's. "So, take less. Just come home. Six months, tops. Not a minute more. They're grown men. Let them figure out how it's done."

I move my face closer, careful not to be seen, or squeak the floor.

"I promise," he says. "I promise."

She leans in to him and lets him stroke her hair. I use the opportunity to back off, turn down the hall.

"But I hate you, now. You should know that . . ." I hear her say, before I close my bedroom door.

As if it were a dream rather than a memory, I forget about it for a few days—the fight, her words, the money, all of it. Or maybe I don't forget so much as block it, once again, from my mind. After all, I may be a lot of crappy things lately, but I want to believe that thief isn't one of them.

At least I hope not.

Then Max comes over again, and this time my mother sends me over the edge.

It's the day the baseball championships are beginning and we have home field advantage, so it's not like we can hang around after school. Aubrey is there, with those girls. Half the school is there.

Max says we should go hang out behind the Hay & Feed where he and his friends ride their dirt bikes after school, but it smells like manure there. Plus, they smoke weed, and Dean's and Bo's girlfriends go sometimes, too, and it's not like they like me, or want some goody-two-shoes sopho-more hanging around.

"How about your house?" I ask like I have before.

"Off-limits, Jailbait, I told you. At least when the old man might be there."

"My mom is a disaster," I offer, tired of always risking

the crap at my house. "She sleeps all the time, and floats around like a ghost in her stupid kimonos."

Max raises his eyebrows up and down like that old comedian with the cigar and bushy mustache, and smiles, and I punch his arm. Like I need to be reminded how hot my mom is. He doesn't get how messed up she is. All I've told him is that she's kind of depressed. It's not exactly the type of thing you share with your new boyfriend, that your mother hallucinates and writes letters to a dead man.

"Your mom may cry and sleep a lot, Jailbait, but my dad is an asshole. Trust me. And your house is a freaking palace compared to mine."

When we get home, Mom is out, the one good thing about her constant, if futile, appointments with Dr. Marsdan.

We go to my room, and fall onto my bed, and make out desperately, till I'm having a hard time stopping myself and Max is practically begging for more.

I roll off the bed and walk to the habitat to let the butterflies out, and we watch them circle for a while, until Max turns on my television and we fall asleep to an episode of some show Max loves called *BoJack Horseman*.

When we finally emerge to get something to eat, Mom is back, sitting in the living room, a book in her hand.

She must have seen Max's dirt bike, but she didn't come find me. Six months ago, she never would have let me stay in my room with a boy with the door closed, not that I had a boyfriend to prove it. There's so much she doesn't seem to bother with anymore.

Her attention doesn't shift as we reach her, which fills me with panic. What if she's in one of her weird trances? I should have made Max leave earlier.

My eyes dart to the kitchen, wondering if I can skirt us

past before Max can take her in, bare legs to her thighs in her lime-green kimono.

"Hello, Mrs. Markham!" Max calls out a little too enthusiastically. He veers toward her, and Mom's head jerks up and she smiles, but her eyes stay glazed and distant.

"Jackie?" She perks up, turning to where Max stands, not seeing me at all.

"Mom . . . It's Max."

She stands and takes a step closer. Max's eyes stay glued to her legs. Of course they are. She may be deluded, but she's half-naked, and beautiful.

"Mom!" I clear my throat. "This is *Max*. Max Gordon. My boyfriend. You know him."

Max looks at me, confused, and I seriously think I'm going to have a heart attack. I look back to Mom and squeak out, "Mom, please"—and her eyes catch mine, and something clicks. My breath returns.

"Of course," she says, nodding.

She closes the book in her hand, drops it on the chair. The cover is white, a paperback with orange and red squares. Black title. *On the Road,* by Jack Kerouac. She's been reading it for weeks. The pile of envelopes flashes through my head: *Jean-Louis Kerouac. Return to Sender.* I haven't asked about my name yet. I can't bring myself to do it.

"Max Gordon," I say again. "You remember Max, Mom, right?"

"Of course I do; don't be silly," my mother says, more assertively now. "Did you tell me he'd be here?" She holds out a hand to shake his, tugging at the hem of her robe with the other like she's realized she's not dressed appropriately, but it's not like there's more fabric to go around.

"No, he wasn't planning to stay . . . We fell asleep . . . We had let the butterflies out and the TV was on, so . . ." But I don't bother finishing because it's not like she cares.

Her eyes snap to mine, so I add, "His bike is outside. I was sure you'd see it."

"Right," she says, focusing on Max. "Well, I'm so pleased to see you again, Maxwell."

Maxwell? She calls him Maxwell like she's morphed into some modern-day Amanda Wingfield, the mother in the play I first read in Hankins' class, the one that led Max to asking me out. *The Glass Menagerie,* it was called, about this girl Laura who has a really bad limp from some disease she had as a child. So, she's basically a recluse, and all she does is listen to old records and play with her prized collection of glass animals.

Max had immediately volunteered to read the part of Tom, Laura's brother, who works in a factory but dreams of being a poet. Raj Thakur was reading for Jim, a work friend of Tom's who comes for dinner and who the mother, Amanda, hopes will fall in love with Laura. At first you think there's no way he will, and anyway Amanda keeps flirting with him, but the two of them do actually go to Laura's room, and they hit it off, and even end up slow dancing, but it turns out Jim is engaged and the whole thing only gets sadder from there.

Anyway, when Hankins announced we'd be reading the play aloud in class, I was shocked when Max volunteered to read for Tom. Like everyone else, I figured Max Gordon was in class because he thought he could fly under the radar in some mindless elective. But it was the opposite. Max would volunteer to read aloud for every play, every sonnet, and he seemed to know half of them by heart. And when I got picked to read for Laura, well, that was in February, and after that, everything between Max and me had escalated.

But now Max stands in my living room ogling my mom,

and he's picked up the book, and they're suddenly going on about Kerouac and how brilliant he was, and so Max seems way more Jim than Tom Wingfield, and all I want is for my mother to shut up, and Max to go home, and this whole nightmare with my mother to be over.

Part II

The courtship dances of some male butterflies may appear aggressive, but they are merely intended to drive competitors away.

The last of the late buses pulls out of the circle revealing no Max, no dirt bike, just a vacant front lot with the sun flooding down onto the concrete, bleaching its already-faded gray to near bone white. Only the ring of baby poplars the school's Sierra Club planted last year on the center mound offers any shade, casting shadows onto the white, an occasional breeze making their leaves rustle up and dance, before falling still.

I walk to the stone wall where I always sit to wait for him, and peel off my sweater and drape it across my bare thighs, letting the warmth spread down my shoulders and back. It's seriously hot for this time of year, at least in this unshaded spot.

I glance at my phone, but there are no texts. It's almost 3:00 p.m. Max should have been here ten minutes ago. Sometimes I get tired of feeling like he forgets I'm alone here, friendless, waiting on him.

Or maybe it's better that he's late, leaving the school grounds mostly empty, and fewer people to witness his public displays of affection.

The heavy steel doors burst open releasing the cavernous darkness of inside into the sunlight. Probably a lingering teacher, still gung ho on being present and available after school, even though all the clubs are basically over.

My stomach sinks when Aubrey walks out with Meghan and Niccole. They're huddled together talking and laughing like co-conspirators.

That used to be us.

If they short-cut to the exit, they'll keep their distance, but if they stay with the curve of the walkway, Aubrey will pass right in front of me.

She doesn't turn, but I know she sees me. Maybe I'll call out, be the one to break the rules of whatever this dumb game is we've been playing. Try to be friendly. After all, it's partly my fault, all this weird distance between us. I've been too caught up with my own stuff—Mom and Max and everything. And my feelings were hurt when Aubrey first started spending more time with those girls and ditched our planned spring elective schedule to have more classes with them than me. And not just Hankins' class, but Forensics instead of Environmental Studies. Suddenly they all had five classes together and Aubrey and I only had two. Both of which those girls are also in. So, I backed away, latched on to Max. Maybe more than I should have.

"Hey, Aubs!" I call softly, before I can overthink it. But they're already past me, veering off the path, and by the time I call her name a second time, more loudly than before, they've reached the end of the driveway, the two metal gates that cars can't slip through after a certain hour, but bodies easily can. "Never mind," I add without waiting. "Have a good night." Only then does Aubrey turn and give me a halfhearted wave.

"Oh, hey, sorry! I didn't see you there," she lies. "We're studying for Stout's test if you want to come."

My heart does this little flip at the possibility, but my

brain knows better. She's being polite. There's no way she wants me to join. Even if she does, the other two girls don't. They make it clear, Niccole leaning in to say something, then throwing her head back in an exaggerated laugh, and Meghan tugging at her arm.

I cut my eyes up to the blue sky, the white puff clouds drifting by. No need to go where I'm not wanted. Besides, Max will be here any minute. So how come tears spring to my eyes?

"Thanks!" I call. "But I'm good."

At that, Niccole laughs a second time, and Aubrey slaps her arm, and then they're in motion again, the occasional burst of laughter drifting back like a knife in my direction.

I lie back on the wall, and stare up at the clouds. When we were in middle school, Aubrey and I once spent a week trying to grasp all the things we didn't understand about the world. Like why the sky is blue, or clouds are white when water is clear, or how sound can travel through telephone wires, or be wrangled and contained when there are no wires at all? Or how the ocean stays in the places it stays instead of all that water spilling over the edge? We knew the answers would be things like the scattering of molecules, or because gravity holds it there, but we really wanted to understand *how*.

But, after days of trying, I still found the answers impossible to comprehend. Each explanation only led to more questions of why or how. Like, the sky is blue because when sunlight reaches the Earth's atmosphere, its light is scattered in all directions by the gases and particles in the air. And blue light is scattered more than other colors because it travels in shorter and smaller waves. But why are those waves shorter, and why does that make it so those are the waves we see?

It all seemed random to me—to us—and ridiculously

hard to hold on to, and for the next few days after that, I felt sad and depressed, until Aubrey decided our next mission was to learn all of the movies that were made into TV shows and I forgot about the more obtuse questions altogether.

I sit up and glance at my phone. Max should have been back twenty minutes ago. I hoist my backpack onto my lap, and rummage for the folder with the US History study packet, my mind wandering to Max, to the money, to my mother. To my father's text message that appeared like kismet a few days ago:

Idea: How about you visit this summer when school is out? Last chance. I'm home for good in September.

How could a month on the beach in Malibu possibly be bad? ☺ Think about it!

I stared at his words, my thoughts racing. I could make this work. Tell a few lies. Say I'm flying in, but travel with Max instead, have him drop me off at LAX when we get there.

Yes. Maybe. Good idea! I wrote back, my heart thrumming with excitement. After all, this was a sign, right? This would make everything possible.

So how come I still hadn't mentioned it to Max?

I slip the packet from the folder. We have a unit test tomorrow, and I'm seriously behind. I turn to the first page, called "The Road to World War One," to the cartoon of Theodore Roosevelt with his walrus mustache and round glasses, and the caption *Big Stick Diplomacy* underneath. But already my mind is back on Max, what it might feel like to have a whole bunch of days alone with him. Just the two of us, on the back of his bike, headed to California. No more Mom and her craziness; no more Nana and her forced cheerfulness; no more Aubrey pretending to give a crap.

Max and me, alone. Two people in love doing whatever we want to.

I put the folder down and lie back again, my mind drifting away from the hard, confusing things to Max and his lips and his hands, and how it feels to have them on me.

My gut lurches at the sound of a car—not Max on his dirt bike—and a horn honking. I roll my head to the side in time to see a shiny red Mustang convertible, circa 2003.

Ethan, swinging around the empty bus circle in my direction.

The U-Haul is already in your driveway when I get there. You insisted I come, insisted I be there to say goodbye to your brother.

And why wouldn't you insist? You have no idea my heart is breaking.

Ethan emerges from the house, carrying armfuls of blankets, pillows, his tennis bag, sneakers tied together and hung over his forearm. His eyes dart sheepishly to mine when he sees me.

"You're just in time to help, JL!" you call happily, waving me over, enthusiastically.

Ethan doesn't say a word.

And you? You don't have a clue.

How could I begin to tell you?

The car stops, idles. The driver-side window rolls down.

"That you, Markham?"

I don't move a muscle. My heart bangs hard in my chest, a crush of emotions nearly obliterating me. Excitement. Panic. Embarrassment. The air, already warm, grows thick and oppressive.

The car is Mr. Andersson's old one, his prized baby he saved for the day Ethan got his license, and let him take to U Penn after he made dean's list his first semester. In it, at the curb across from where I sit, Ethan squints up at me, into the sunlight.

"Hey! It *is* you, right?"

Does he have to keep asking? Who does he think it is?

I try to smile, but it's forced like some plastered-on Joker's grin. The memories rush back: his basement, the orange chair, the game of chicken in the pool . . . Images I'd tried to forget, not because I wanted to, but because I needed to.

He lowers the passenger-side window the rest of the way and says, "It *is* you. I thought so," and he gives a big smile, like it's all okay. Like it's all normal, when it so totally isn't. Like none of the things that happened mattered. Good old, reliable Ethan. Aubrey hadn't told me he was back already.

Why would she have? We barely speak. And, anyway, even if we did, why would she think I'd care?

"Hey, Ethan," I finally manage. I sit up and swing my legs over the edge but don't move off the wall. He can come to me if he wants. And he won't. I used to think he would, but I don't anymore.

"That's it? 'Hey, Ethan'? I don't see you for months and that's all you have for me? I came to collect my sister, but it's better to find you waiting here."

I'm not waiting for you, *jerk,* I want to say, but I don't even know why I'm mad at him. He was leaving for college, and I'm his sister's best friend. So, he left, and didn't turn back. What was he supposed to do? Besides, I'm with Max now.

Still, that it all seems light and easy for him bothers me, when everything since that night has been hard for me. The feeling bad. The guilt. The missing him and not being able to tell.

Until Max came along and helped me forget everything.

"You mad at me?" Ethan cups a hand to his eyes to block the sun and waits, but I sit mute, because I don't know the answer to his question.

Am I mad at him, or something worse than that?

Crushed.

Heartbroken.

But not anymore. I have Max. Whatever happened with Ethan is ancient history.

"Saturday night," you say. "It's going to be ah-mazing."

"And you're sure we're invited?" I ask, tentatively.

"Of course we are. It's my brother. Combo graduation–bon voyage party."

You tell me to come early, so we can plan our outfits and mix-and-match bikinis—not that the slew of graduated seniors will give a crap about us, fresh out of ninth grade. But you're giddy with excitement. It's not like your parents normally allow this stuff, turning a blind eye to the keg they know Ethan plans to hide in the bushes.

"It's weird," you say. "I think my father is helping him. They're not themselves, my parents. Either of them. It's like they've gone all soft because he's leaving and they want his last few days at home to be super-fun." You roll your eyes. "As if my parents could ever be the cool ones."

But your mom is sure trying. By the time I get there at six, she's drinking wine and dancing around the kitchen in her long, striped pool cover-up to the music Ethan already has blasting in the yard, trays of mini hot dogs spread across the kitchen counter.

"No chance she's awake past ten p.m.," you whisper, as you sneak me past the kitchen and up the stairs to your room.

———

By 9:00 p.m., the party is in full swing, the music so loud, I can't believe the neighbors haven't called the cops. Then again, everyone knows and loves your brother, don't they? Eagle Scout, honor roll, varsity tennis champ, Ethan Andersson.

You and I walk out to the backyard. It's thick with bodies, sweaty guys in swim trunks playing volleyball with girls in skimpy bikinis, couples against trees making out, kids in the pool. Still others who have wandered off to the basement to play Ping-Pong and video games.

I barely recognize your mom's perfectly manicured yard with its tent and tables and streamers and lanterns and mostly catered food, even a giant ice sculpture of tennis rackets crossed over each other, lit in purple and blue that, much to your father's later unhappiness, intentionally or unintentionally, doubles as a luge for shots of Jack Daniel's poured from bottles hidden in various spots around the yard.

At the moment, the luge is unattended and your dad is happily chatting with two pretty girls, your mother in the chair next to him, sipping what might be her third or fourth glass of red wine.

"Jesus, they're lame, way to ruin a party," you say, grabbing my hand. "On the other hand, now's our chance," and you pull me toward the kitchen, closing the sliding glass door behind us. Leaving me there, standing guard, you fetch a bottle of red wine from the fridge, pour two big paper cups, hold the bottle under the tap for a second, and swirl it around before shoving it back in behind others on the shelf. You summon me with a raised cup, and I raise my eyebrows in response, so you add, "Hopefully they'll be too wasted to even notice."

Up in your room, we sip at the wine and change into our new bikinis we bought for the occasion—one purple and white stripes, the other green paisley—and we each take half, and admire ourselves, tipsy opposites, in the mirror.

You cup your chest in your hands, push up, and say, "You look bigger; maybe I should take the striped top," and without missing a beat, I whip it off and hand it to you, and you strip off your bottoms and we switch, so that now we're opposites once again, smiling at each other in the mirror.

"You really would do anything for me, wouldn't you?" you say, and I bust out laughing, though I'm not sure why. It's like a bunch of mixed emotions are swirling inside me and coming out as uncontrollable laughter: I feel happy and giddy and excited and nervous and guilty and sad all at the same time. Maybe it's the wine. You do another spin, locate your cup, and down the rest impossibly fast.

"Finish yours, too," you order. I oblige, and lie down next to you where you've collapsed backward on your bed.

"I love you, JL," you say, finding and holding my hand, and stretching one foot up in the air, your blue-polished toes pointed toward the ceiling. "Hey, remember that?" You draw a circle with your toes around a shadow of splatter on the ceiling.

"Mr. Popper's Pepsi," I say. "Our TV commercial phase."

You drop your leg and laugh. "Mr. Popper's Pepsi will pop your taste buds wide open," you say, putting on the too-perky voice you used that day. "Personally, I prefer it!"

"Pop one today!" I say, extricating my hand from yours to pretend to pull a pop-top can open in the air above me. "And that's when I jumped down from the bed and . . ." I make an explosion with my hands. "Who knew soda could reach that far?"

"We were so scared, remember? But my parents never found out."

I close my eyes and smile. The wine is making the room spin a little, the dizziness mixing with good memories of us little, doing dumb, carefree things. It feels like so long ago since I felt like a kid, like you and I could be light and silly, and play pretend. The real world and high school have been so much harder.

"Should we go down?" I ask, my brain skirting for the first time since I got here to Ethan, where I promised I wouldn't let it go. "Aubs?"

You don't answer, and I nudge you. "Aubrey!"

But you're asleep. Snoring deeply.

Your parents are no longer in the chairs by the pool and I didn't pass them in the kitchen, so maybe they're watching a movie in the living room, or upstairs. Or maybe they went to bed. But doubtful with the party still going on.

There are way more people out here than earlier when we headed up to your room. I feel stupid without you, unsure what to do. Maybe I should go home. Thoughts of Ethan noticing me, or caring if he did, are all but vanished. I've already spotted him—off in the corner laughing with a pretty brunette with a better body than I'll ever have, named Carly Witherspoon.

My heart sinks. Even her name is sophisticated.

Emboldened by the buzz from the wine, I walk over to the keg and hold a red Solo cup under the tap, my eyes scanning for your parents, who would likely kill me, or at least send me home, which wouldn't be the worst thing. What's the point of staying here, anyway?

"Can I see your ID?" There's a hand on my shoulder and I startle, but it's just Dante Darby, who you have a crush on.

Did you know he would be here?

My eyes shoot to your window, but the lights are still off, how I left them. I wonder for a brief moment if I should run back up and try to wake you.

"Hey, Dante," I say, staring down at the trickle of liquid in my cup. "Aubrey crashed on me early. It was probably the wine. Anyway, I was just thinking how I should probably go home."

"Getting a beer for the road, then?" I shrug and he takes my cup and fills it, and hands it back to me. "Kidding. Stay. Really. We were about to play chicken and you're dressed for it, and we need teams. Half these bozos didn't wear a bathing suit to a pool party." He eyes me in my new bikini in a way that makes me wonder if he's interested, but it's a stupid thought, and anyway, I'd never do that to you. *Never.* Then again, I seem unable to stop pining for Ethan, which is worse and gross and horrible, and I know you'd so totally never forgive me.

"Okay," I say, my eyes scanning the crowd, but Ethan has disappeared, probably off in the bushes with Carly.

I sit by the pool with Dante, listening to him tell me his whole long college application story, which is even more boring than it sounds, and waiting for a game to start up, but by 11:00 p.m. the crowd is starting to thin and there's no game of chicken to be found.

Ethan is to be found, though—back from wherever he disappeared to—and not with Carly Witherspoon, who seems to have, thankfully, gone home.

By 11:30, I've had at least two more beers, and Ethan comes over with another, and tells Dante to scoot, and suddenly he's sitting right next to me.

It's then I realize how out of control my brain feels. Like the earth is spinning right up and out from under me.

To tell you the truth, Aubrey, I liked how it felt, to be all dizzy and free like that. Maybe I felt like my mother in that moment, like I wanted to spin and whirl with my kimono falling open, my molecules loosening inside, till I spilled breathless and sprawled onto the dew-dampened grass, my limbs splayed dangerously wide, my whole beautiful body—its bare, uncovered skin—glistening beneath the star-dotted sky.

I liked how it felt to be out of control, a moth on a carnival ride, ready to be swept off by the wind, every tenuous hair, every fiber, every quivering speck of me, lit up, on end, and electrified.

Someone has thrown someone in the pool, and Ethan takes off running, and dives into the deep end. When he surfaces at the side, he calls to me.

"Hey, Markham! Come in! Now! You're on my team. The water is fine!"

I make my way over, aware of the light, and smells, and sounds, as if all my senses are firing, both sharp and blurred by the swirl of alcohol. The waffle of water reflecting across the yard from the pool light, slicing across the high tree branches like specters. The swish of my feet in wet grass. A breeze on my stomach. The trill of crickets in the space between hushed shouts that rise in the nearly autumn air.

"We have to keep it down," Ethan says. "I don't want my parents to come out."

A girl named Shamika teams up with some kid named Randy, and a girl named Mariah teams up with Dante, and I feel a little better about you missing this since she's not nearly as pretty as you.

Ethan pushes water aside as he wades to the shallow end

steps, and holds out his hand for me. "Come on, slowpoke. I'm going to need you to get in fast and climb up here."

My heart beats overtime as he turns his back to me, his broad, tanned shoulders waiting for me to climb on, my legs now straddling his neck. He wraps his hands around my thighs, pulling me against him.

"Hold on tight," he says, parading forward.

And we're in motion, a frenzy of splashing and laughing, and hushing each other, and tugging, and parading, and bodies falling, tangled, into the water, then scrambling to get back up.

At first, Ethan is tentative with me, but as the game gets more raucous, his hands slide higher up my thighs, squeezing my ass. I find myself breath holding as I wait for each new place he might inadvertently touch me. My butt, my waist, my back. I want to feel him there, holding me. I want the current that runs beneath the surface of the water to explode like lightning up through his body and into mine.

More than that, I want the pool and the game and the remaining partygoers to all disappear, and for Ethan to carry me out of the pool and onto the grass, and crawl on top of me, and have his way with me.

Granted, I'm not sure what this means, and granted, I know it's wrong, but I don't care. I can hardly breathe thinking about how much I want it all.

When someone announces it's almost 1:00 a.m., we finally get out, and stand around waiting for the last, exhausted dregs of life to be sucked from the party, from your backyard, from the keg, for the parents to pick everyone up, or designated drivers to sort out who they can fit in their cars, and Ethan comes over to where I stand, more than drunk, desperate with wanting, shivering in a towel by the fence.

"You okay, Markham?"

"Yeah. Just a little tired and cold." His eyes bore through me in the dark, in the haze of the moon.

"You should go inside."

I want to scream, *No!* I want to wrap his arms around my body, I want to re-catch the lightning in a bottle that minutes ago I was so sure was us, in the pool.

He takes off his towel and drapes it over me, pulling me toward him. I look at him, my eyes surely pleading, trying to tell him.

The air hums, silent but alive.

"You know I need to kiss you," he says.

My breath releases. "You do?"

"Yes. Badly. For a long time."

I try to say no for you, Aubrey; I do. I want to. I think the word, *No,* loudly in my head. Urgently. But what comes out instead is, "I want you to."

And like that we're kissing, and he's moving me backward into the shadows of the bushes, and his hands are on me, in my hair, down my back, in the fabric of my bikini top, everywhere.

It's delirious. I'm delirious. The air swirls. My legs feel boneless, so I can barely stay upright.

I think I'm fucking in love with him.

"Can I?"

I nod, and whisper, "Anything," and he opens my towel, and pushes in against me, and kisses my lips again, and lets the towel fall to the ground, his mouth moving down to my collarbone, his fingers pulling my bikini top aside so his lips brush the skin of my nipples, before moving down my stomach toward my bottoms. And the whole time he's saying things like, "Jesus, Markham, you're beautiful," and, "You sure it's okay? You have no idea how long I've wanted to . . ." and I'm nodding without breath, and figuring out how to keep upright.

"I love you, Ethan," I say without meaning to, and hear his name again, "Ethan," in my ears, except the second time it isn't me, my voice, my words. It's coming from elsewhere, but he doesn't hear it.

"Ethan," I say, urgently this time, yanking him back up, and checking his face in the moonlight, in the darkness, because I need to—because before it's all over, I want to be sure.

"Yeah?" he says, confused, but then he hears it, too, and says, "Oh shit, oh Jesus. I'm so sorry, Markham."

Except I don't want him to be sorry. I don't want him to stop, or leave, or worry about who is coming, except we have to, even if I want this, it, *us,* to keep going.

"Ethan? You out here?" The voice grows closer and I try to focus on the pool through the trees, but the air is spinning and the yard is spinning, and I want to cry at how his mouth is gone from mine. "Ethan!" His name louder, in our direction.

Your mother, Aubrey.

Your mother.

"Out here, Mom!" Ethan calls, trying to make his voice sound normal. "We're cleaning up." He pushes me back, grabbing the towel from the ground and holding it up as some sort of proof of I don't know what, as we move out from behind the bushes. "Kids left stuff everywhere. JL was helping. I'll get this whole mess cleaned up before morning."

Your mother's eyes are on me, suspicious, taking in the scene. I have nothing in my hands to show I was helping. I didn't have that kind of time to think.

There is nothing to indicate I'm innocent.

"Shouldn't you be home, JL?" Your mom's words are sharp, scolding. "Mr. Andersson can drive you. It's way too late to walk alone."

I could sleep here, I want to say. *I always sleep here.* But I don't. I can't. I've betrayed you, and your mother is rightfully sending me home.

My eyes dart to Ethan for help, for solace, for him to stand up for me, declare his love for me—anything—but he's busy picking up cups and napkins and empties, as your mother disappears across the lawn.

And then the U-Haul is in your driveway, and Ethan is shoving his stuff into the back. And if you ever find out what happened, Aubrey, you'll kill me. You'll never want to be my friend again. And with my dad still gone, and my mother seeming more and more ill by the minute, I can't lose you, too. I just can't.

When the last of his possessions are stuffed in the truck, Ethan's eyes catch mine for one split second, and he says, "That's it, I think. Everything I need is loaded up."

And I know right then, there is not a single person in the whole wide world solid enough to rely on.

No one, Aubrey.

Not even myself.

"I take it that's a yes?" Ethan moves his grip on the steering wheel, drumming his fingers on the dashboard to the turned-down music. "You're mad at me," he clarifies, as if his understanding of the obvious is what makes it so.

He turns the car off, and pulls the key from the ignition. I trace the rays of sunlight from his hair, to his cheek, to his fingers, trying to block out the flashes of shoved-away things.

The pool.

Me, on his shoulders.

His lips.

His tongue in my mouth. Down my stomach . . .

"No. Not mad." I want this to be true. "Distracted. Preoccupied. Overwhelmed." I search for words, but none of them seem right. They all sound like lies set loose.

"So I see." It's not clear at first that he's teasing me, being sarcastic, but then he motions around the empty parking lot and laughs. I'm tempted to blurt out about Max, how I'm waiting for him, how every day, practically, he meets me here, how his hands have been all over me, too. How I'm going to sleep with him the minute I turn sixteen. How I'm going to California with him.

Max Gordon will be here soon, so you might want to leave,

I want to say. *Max Gordon who hates you. Who pretty much hates all you Anderssons.*

"They think they're too good for everyone," Max once told me when I was complaining how Aubrey had ditched me. "I could do circles around them, and not just in an open field on my bike. Give me any class, any test. On the fucking APs if I wanted to. But some of us don't have anything to prove."

Now I wonder if that's true, Aubrey. If there's anyone who doesn't have something to prove.

Ethan opens the car door, and strolls toward me.
Shit.

I busy myself slipping the study packet into my backpack, and try to find something normal to say, opting for the inane, "So, you're home for the summer already?" when he reaches me.

"Yeah, last week." He places his hand down on the concrete wall next to me, flat, open fingers, and I want to trace each one, touch him for a second. It's been more than eight months since I've seen him. "Penn finishes early. I'm surprised I haven't seen you around?" It's a question accompanied by a look of concern, which only makes me madder. I guess Aubrey hasn't told him about Max, about how she and I aren't really that great of friends anymore, about how much has changed since he left for school. I count the weeks back in my head since the butterflies arrived. I haven't been to their house in almost two months. "Don't you usually *live* at our place?" he asks.

I shift my gaze to him, focusing not on his face but the strands of blond hair lit gold in the sunshine, on the small crescent scar on his forehead he got in sixth grade. I think of that day, how we were all riding our bikes in the rain, down by the creek in the woods behind Holly White's house. Ethan hit a rock and fell, and smashed his head on a downed tree limb. I didn't give a crap about Ethan Andersson then. He was just my new best friend's nerdy older brother. In my head, I trace the physical path back from the Whites' house to our cul-de-sac, anything to keep my mind from wandering.

Besides, why all the concern from Ethan now? I haven't heard from him since he left for school. Not on breaks, not in texts, not for anything. Not when overachieving Ethan Andersson decided to skip Christmas break to do a J-term in the Sudan, or over Thanksgiving break—which was short and the only one he came home for—the Anderssons busy with their relatives and us busy with my father home, which was mostly stupid chaos.

"The Sudan? Are you kidding me?" I had asked Aubrey after Thanksgiving, when she first mentioned Ethan was planning on it. "Like, isn't that dangerous? Isn't there a war going on there?" And we had both rolled our eyes, because that was so like good old Ethan. But unlike Aubrey, I was pretending. I was worried, and more than desperate for him to come home, and for me to have a chance to see him.

"You know my brother," Aubrey had finally said, shrugging. "Mr. Social Justice. He'll be okay, though. Good riddance."

Good riddance. Right.

"Markham?" Ethan breaks through my thoughts.

"Yeah." If he really cared, in all those months he would have reached out to me.

He turns his back to me and I think he's going to leave, but he reaches up and hauls himself next to me on the wall. My heart pounds so hard, I'm sure he's going to be able to hear its insane drumbeat filling the few inches of sweltering air between us. He bumps my shoulder with his. "You sure everything is okay, kid?"

Kid.

"Yeah, why?" I sound so obviously like the liar I am. I should blurt something—anything real and honest—even if it's stupid, about my mother getting worse by the hour, about Dad renewing his California contract yet again. About the rift between Aubrey and me. I've known Ethan forever. Whatever happened between us, I don't hate him. I shouldn't be afraid to tell him what's going on.

Besides, if I don't tell him something soon, and get him out of here, Max is going to show up, and wrap his arms around me, and say something obnoxious to Ethan to humiliate me. A trickle of sweat slips down between my shoulder blades.

"Okay, I'll leave you be, I guess," he says. "I just figured when I saw you, you'd know where Aubrey is. Got a clue where that sister of mine has gone to?"

"No," I say. "As a matter of fact, I don't." A lump settles in my throat making it hard to swallow.

"Really? How come?" I shrug, because now I can't get any words out without crying. "Well, she has a dentist appointment and I'm supposed to retrieve her and deliver her there. If you see her, she apparently forgot. So let her know."

"Will do," I say, and he reaches his arm around my shoulder and gives me a squeeze.

"It really is good to see you, Markham," he says.

I close my eyes against tears and the dizzying swirl, but that only makes it worse, so I snap them open and blurt, "She's at Meghan Riley's house with Niccole Saunders, where else?" I nod in the direction they walked off. "Her new best friends. Meghan lives over on that short street off Burberry? You know it? The dead end. Call Aubrey's cell. I'm sure you'll reach her."

He turns and gives me that same intense look he gave me earlier, like he's super-worried, then shakes his head as if it's none of his business. But he was leaving a minute ago, and he's still sitting here now, and I don't have a clue what to do.

"It sure is weird to be back in this place, you know?" he says after a few seconds of silence. "Like you can never go home again, or something like that." He kicks the wall with his tennis shoe, and it occurs to me I don't even know if he's still playing or not, whether he sits or gets on the court. I don't know how the Sudan was. I don't know anything. I should ask him. About classes and sports and stuff, about wherever the hell it was he went last December.

"Yeah, more than you know," I say instead, but my words barely come out. I stare out past his car to the center mound. The poplar leaves catch a soft gust making their gray shadows shimmy on the ground. I glance at my cell, wondering where Max is; if, mercifully, he decided not to come.

"You'd better go get your sister," I say. "I forgot the reception sucks around here lately. Even if you text her, she may not get it. It's the big blue house at the end of that block."

"Okay," he says. "I could give you a lift home?"

The question holds hope, or maybe just worry.

"No, I'm good. Turns out, I'm waiting for someone."

"Oh?" He raises an eyebrow, and I want to laugh, or maybe punch him. Tell him to go fuck himself. Does he think he's the only guy who ever liked me?

"Yeah, I'm good here," I say, and wait for him to put an end to all this misery.

"Well, okay, then." He moves toward his car, and I breathe a sigh of relief. But at the driver's side he stops and turns, and walks all the way back toward me.

"You know you can talk to me, Markham."

But he's wrong. I don't know that. I don't know it at all. In fact, I don't know anything. I close my eyes to stop the tears from spilling over. It's all so dumb. None of it matters anymore. I don't want or need any help from Ethan Andersson.

The sound of a bike engine revving, picking up speed, rounding the bend, fills the air. And the sight of Max Gordon follows.

Max, like some crazy derelict, zipping in through the far side of the parking lot, toward us.

"Come on, Wingfield. Follow me." Max has been calling me this—Wingfield—ever since we read *The Glass Menagerie*.

It's smart and sounds like a name on a sports jersey, so I adore it.

It's freezing out, and Max is clearly insane for taking us down to the water, which shouldn't surprise me; it's basically what I've been told about him from anyone who knows him in our grade. "Max Gordon is crazy." "Max Gordon is an alcoholic." "Max Gordon is a total dog." All those things have proven untrue, but I still should have known better than to agree to get on the back of his dirt bike and go down to the shore on the cusp of night with him. Especially here, on this unlit beach in the middle of nowhere.

I shiver, and pull my coat tighter, rewrapping my scarf around my face to keep the wind from numbing my forehead. My hands are frozen. I stupidly forgot my gloves.

Max takes my hand. His fingers are warm. He only wears a sweatshirt, but doesn't seem cold.

"Here, down this way," he says. "There's a path, I think. If I know where I am." I stumble, and Max catches me. "Hold on, I'll use a light." He pulls his phone from his pocket and shines the harsh glare ahead of us, illuminating tangles of brambles and bare branches. "Guess it's over-grown some since I was here last," he adds.

He kicks away stuff with his boot, and sure enough, underfoot is a path, and soon everything opens up to soft sand and moonlit water. I stop and stare out, and he moves behind me, and wraps his arms around me, pulling me tight against him. My stomach drops. I'm pretty sure I'm about to make out with Max Gordon. Maybe now I'll stop thinking about Ethan once and for all.

"I'm glad you came with me, Wingfield. I would have bet money you wouldn't have come. Not in a million years."

"Yeah, well, I probably shouldn't have," I mumble through the warm, damp wool of my scarf. Bits of fibers stick in my mouth and I want to reach up and move it away, but my arms are pinned by his embrace. My stomach lurches again, knowing I'm out here alone with him. He could do any-thing he wanted. I'm fifteen, and no one knows where I am. I shouldn't have lied to my mom.

I wriggle free and turn to face him, a little terrified, but also exhilarated. Of course he won't do that. He seems to like me.

"I'm probably going to die of frostbite," I say, and he loosens his grip, and pulls my scarf down off my mouth, runs his thumb over my lower lip and says, "What was that you said?"

"Frostbite," I repeat. "You and me, here, frozen to death. Two blocks of ice in a snowbank."

"Nope," he says. "I wouldn't let that happen. And any-way, you're wrong. Fire, not ice." He slides his thumb back and forth over my lip, making a current run through me, from my mouth down my body, beneath my coat.

"Huh?" I whisper.

He leans in and places his warm lips over mine. The

kiss is so soft. So tender. It's everything. When he straightens, he looks me in the eyes.

"'Some say the world will end in fire, Some say in ice.'" His thumb is back on my lip, the touch melting me even more than the kiss, so maybe he's right. "'From what I've tasted of desire I hold with those who favor fire.' So, see?" His mouth brushes mine, less gentle, a bit more insistent. So good, my legs are trembling. I have no idea what he's said, but I don't care. His words thrill me. He thrills me. I've never felt this ready for anything—ever—in my whole life.

MID-MAY
TENTH GRADE

Max slows when he sees me—sees Ethan—stopping several yards from us, straddling the still-idling bike. Despite its low hum, the air hangs silent, a distant high-pitched ringing in my ears.

"What's that douchebag doing here?" Ethan asks. "No worries, I'll get rid of him."

Aubrey definitely hasn't told him anything.

"Ethan, wait—"

He turns, must catch my tone, whatever look is on my face, because he says, "Oh, geez. Tell me that's not who you're waiting for?" I don't answer. "Seriously, Markham? That asshole?"

"He's not an asshole." I want to scream, but instead I barely say it loud enough for him to hear. But I should. I should tell Ethan how smart Max is, how he recites sonnets to me, how even Hankins likes him, and how Max has stuck by me for almost three months, which is more than I can say for everyone else who says they care. But I don't. Max doesn't need defending. Not by me. And not *to* Ethan. Not to anyone.

Ethan turns toward Max, and back to me, his face still twisted with confusion.

"We're dating," I clarify. "Since February. I figured your

nosy sister might have told you." I sound mad. Defensive. I guess maybe I am.

I walk toward the curb, and Max finally takes off his helmet, steps away from his bike, and walks to me. His hair is matted with sweat, his step heavy in his jeans, in this heat, and his lumberjack boots. His scruffy face wears a look of something I can't exactly define, hurt, maybe, mixed with defiance, and a hint of, "I might have to kick your ass."

Ethan, in his tennis shorts and pale mint polo, looks baby-faced and insignificant.

"That's a fact, Andersson," Max says, moving toward Ethan intentionally, veering away at the last second as he walks past. "We're together, JL and me. I take it you don't have an issue with that?" Max's voice, the words he chooses, loose in the air, how he calls me by my name rather than one of his nicknames, all sound less weird and disjointed than I worried they would. They actually sound romantic and beautiful.

When he reaches me, he drapes both arms across my shoulders, and leans in to kiss me. His lips taste like sweat and dust, and the faint hint of a pungent-sweet smoke. "Sorry," he says, "Lost track of time. Not to mention, took a spill. Dean and me had a little collision on the bikes."

Finally, I notice the smear of tan dirt up his leg by his hip, and the red bruise on his cheek.

"Yikes, you okay?"

"Sure," he says. "No biggie. I would have texted, but this piece of junk ran out of charge." He waves his phone at me, and shoves it back in his pocket. "You ready to get out of here?"

I nod.

"Well, good for you guys," Ethan says. I almost forgot he is standing there.

"Good to see you, Ethan," I say. The words burn my throat. They make me kind of sad, too, but I mean them.

He walks to his car, and turns when he reaches his door.

"Hey, Max," he calls, "be good to her, okay?" He gives me one last look before climbing into the driver's seat and taking off.

"Pompous dickwad," Max says when he's gone. He buries his face in my neck and I take in the sweaty, smoky smell of his hair, of his jacket, and try to swallow past the lump in my throat that, lately, doesn't ever seem to go away.

LATE MAY
TENTH GRADE

"Not a dirt bike, Jailbait," Max corrects me, "the Kawa-saki. At least once I get it fixed."

We're sitting on the floor of my room, my back pressed against him, body slipped into the vee of his open legs, watching the butterflies. He revs his lips like an engine, and puts his hands on my shoulders, steering them like handle-bars, making me laugh. "This guy gave it to me cheap. It's fast and powerful, but it needs a complete overhaul. When I'm done, it'll have a four-stroke engine, six-speed trans-mission. You can't ride a dirt bike three thousand miles to California." I tip my head back to look at him, and he combs his fingers through my hair before grasping it into a fisted ponytail to keep it held back. "Jesus, you're fucking beautiful," he says, kissing my forehead, and my nose, and my lips.

"How much will it cost?" I ask, sitting up straight, turn-ing myself to look at him. Two of the Jezebels are out of the habitat and circle the room, their wings catching bits of light that filter in through the half-open shades. They alight on the windowsill, drawn to the warmth of the sun-baked wood.

"I could get a crap one for like four hundred, if I wanted.

A mint one for under a grand. Depends what I want to put inside her. You still need to see her. She deserves the very best."

I nod, my mind skirting to the pink metal boxes that have been stuck in my head, the ones I saw Mom shoving handfuls of bills into the morning after the fight she and Dad had the night of the Rainbow Room.

"There's also the issue of the transmission," Max adds, "and gas, and motels, I guess, if you come with me. Otherwise, I'll crash at a campsite, or on the side of a highway. I don't give a shit." He chuckles like he doesn't believe for a minute I'll go with him.

But more and more lately, my head fills with the salty scent of the ocean, the image of me on the back of Max's bike, arms clutched around his waist, the wind blowing our hair as we breeze past wheat fields, traveling miles and miles of open highway.

"On the road, just the two of us, imagine it!" Max said when I first said I was, maybe, in fact, considering it.

Of course, it's ridiculous to think I can, and I know it. It's a joke. I'm a joke. The idea is a total joke. I've barely been on the back of Max's dirt bike—only from school to here—let alone on a four-something, six-whatever engine thing he's talking about riding across country. Besides, crazy or not, never in a million years would my mother let me go. Forget about Nana or Dad.

And yet there are ways—and a ripening alibi and money to execute it all—that have taken up residence in my brain. And the crazier Mom seems, and the more I fall in love with Max, and the further away Aubrey drifts, the less I can think of one good reason to stay here.

"Why do you ask, Jailbait?"

"Ask what?"

"How much it would cost?"

"No reason." I shrug, and shake the thoughts away, watching a Glasswing emerge and lift off, flying directly at Max, landing on his shoulder for the first time since they've been let out while he's here. "Don't touch it," I whisper, as he reaches up. He yanks his hand back, except it's only a myth that a butterfly will die from someone touching its wing.

"Sorry, I didn't realize."

"Never mind. It's okay." I reach over, and trace the wine-red edge of the butterfly's wing, and it crawls away from my touch toward Max's chest.

It doesn't want to leave him, either.

"They're going to start dying soon, I bet. I'm not even sure how long these guys live. The Jezebels can live longer, at least longer than most. Sometimes up to three months," I say, "but not necessarily."

"How long has it been?" Max asks, lying down carefully, and folding his arms behind his head to watch the Glasswing that stands on his chest rubbing its legs.

"It's tasting you," I say. "They taste with their feet. Middle of April is when they emerged." I try not to count the weeks. It breaks my heart to think of them dying here, of finding them, one after another, lying motionless on the bottom of the habitat. With the Monarchs and Swallowtails, I never had to worry, or witness it, just set them free in the yard after they hatched. Sometimes, a few days later, I'd see one flying about and be sure it was this one or that.

"I'd like you to taste me," Max says, and I swat him, making the Glasswing take off. "Seriously, though, it's cool. I hope they don't die anytime soon."

"Me too," I say, but my mind is racing. If they're still alive when we go to California, who will take care of them?

Better if they go first. It's not like Mom or Nana will be talking to me.

After Max leaves, I walk through the empty house deciding, turning down the hall to Mom's bedroom, telling myself I'm not doing anything wrong.

I'm not doing anything at all.

Just investigating.

Just finding out if it's still there.

At her bedroom door, I change my mind and turn back to my room.

I'm sure it's gone. I'm sure she's burned through it all.

"I kissed him, you know," Nana says, as she moves her wrinkled finger across the monochrome face of Jack Kerouac. She tips her head back and closes her eyes, as if she's trying to better remember it.

The three of us are on the couch in the living room, Nana in the middle, feet up on the coffee table, the big glossy book called *The Beat Generation* she bought Mom open across her lap.

"He was nearing forty by then."

"Robbing the cradle!" Mom says, as if there's some glee in it.

Nana laughs and nods in agreement.

"Gross," I say, rolling my eyes as she turns the page, leaning her head against Mom's for a second. They've always been close, and it makes me long for a time when I felt close to my mother. I did once. At least sort of. But everything's been different since Dad left. Even before the depression morphed into something worse, making her strange and deluded and distant.

Although there are times she still seems normal, like her usual self, which only serves to trick me into thinking everything might be okay.

"Oh, yes, she would have murdered me, if she knew!"

Nana says, and I realize I missed some sort of question from my mother. "My mother was quite proper. You remember her. Can you imagine if she had found out?" Nana fans the air, and Mom laughs, turning more pages.

"Now him," Nana says, making her stop at a photograph of a man with glasses and dark curly hair, a cigarette held in his hand. Behind him, a woman looks wistfully off into the distance. "This is Allen Ginsberg. They were dear, dear friends. Wrote letters to each other for a decade. They're all compiled in a book, I believe."

Even if I don't know who they're talking about, or care all that much if I do, I still feel happy for this evening of normalcy, them giggling together over this dumb book of photos, like you and I might over something on YouTube or Instagram. Everything momentarily feels like it was when I was little. Back when Nana would come over with Pop-pop, and all of us would play Scrabble, and Nana would tell stories from Mom's childhood, Pop-pop complaining that she was exaggerating, and giving looks to my dad like he understood.

"Oh, don't listen to them!" Nana would say, winking at me. "Your mother was a wild child before she met your father. You tamed her," she'd tease Dad. "She got that from me."

Then Pop-pop would laugh, and shake his head, and say that Nana's fond memories of things were far more exciting than any reality that either she or my mother ever lived. He'd add that Mom was lucky to find Dad, and Nana was lucky to find him, to keep them both from floating away into their fantasy lands.

"Well, think what you want, but I did, too, kiss him," Nana would insist, swatting Pop-pop's chest, before wrapping her arms around his neck. "You're supposed to take my side. You're supposed to make me sound at least as exciting as I am."

"I miss Pop-pop; don't you?" my mother asks, suddenly wistful, as if she and I were thinking about the same thing.

"More than ever," Nana answers, softly. "We shouldn't take them for granted. There's something to be said for a practical man." She flips another page, tapping a photo of Kerouac standing outside against a brick wall, a book under one arm, pulling a cigarette to or from his mouth with the other hand. "This one, though," she says, sighing deeply, "that one time, what a thrill."

And Mom tips her head back and says, "Go on, tell me again."

It's a Tuesday evening and Gunther's Tap Room in North-port, Long Island, is dead. Maybe three tables in the whole place are occupied.

My parents have brought me here on a weeknight to celebrate in official fashion.

"A Bud, on tap, for me," my father tells the waitress when she arrives, "and two old-fashioneds for the ladies." The waitress requests my ID, and I hand her the license I pull from my purse. Until now, I've never been asked, but I've never ordered liquor before.

The room is quiet until someone mercifully puts some quarters in the jukebox. "It's Now or Never" comes on, Elvis' deep and syrupy voice and the click of the clave causing me to sway in my seat while we wait.

"Slainte!" my father says, when the waitress returns. He raises his mug into the air. I finger the highball glass the waitress has placed in front of me. Two cubes, a pretty orange-gold liquid the color of apricot, and a toothpick spearing two bright red cherries. Condensation slips like raindrops down the outside of the glass, and I move my finger up its side, drawing the initials "R.C. + B.M." inside a heart, and wiping it away before anyone can notice.

Bobby Masters. He and I had gone steady all through

high school, and last month, citing college in Massachusetts, he had unceremoniously dumped me. I would have gone with him if he had only asked. Instead, I've spent the weeks in tears and, until last week, could barely get out of bed.

My mother, on the other hand, has a hard time hiding how pleased she is, since he wasn't Jewish, a fact she pointed out to me repeatedly during all four years of our romance. I don't have the energy to point out that neither is Dad. It doesn't much matter now.

"Happy birthday, sweetheart," my father says.

"Go ahead, take a sip, Ruthie," my mother chimes in. She must be desperate for me to stop playing the sad sack if she's encouraging me to drink. "And you slow down, mister," she aims at my father. "I don't need you putting on a show." My father is a loud and boisterous drunk, the polar opposite of my mother. As if to demonstrate, she puts her own glass down and dabs demurely at the corners of her lips. It will take her the whole night to finish one drink. Already Dad has finished his beer and is holding up a finger to order another.

My mother gives him a sideways glance.

I want to kill myself. This is my eighteenth birthday.

"Don't be such a spoilsport, Miriam. We're celebrating."

I lift the glass and take a sip. The liquid is warm and sweet, and goes down easy enough, so I take a second, and third, and a few more. To slow myself down, I pull the toothpick from the glass and suck a whiskey-soaked cherry from it. An old-fashioned, then. My new favorite thing.

It's not the first time I've had alcohol, but there is something different about drinking legally, aboveboard. Being of age. And this concoction tastes particularly delicious. I quickly find myself smiling, flushed with a rush that spreads from my chest to my stomach, and mixes with the undeniable pleasure of irking my mother.

This is better, this being a grown-up thing. To hell with high school. To hell with Bobby Masters.

I down the rest of the drink, and my father holds up my empty glass to the light and gives me an approving look. "Shall we order you another?," he asks, which causes my mother to get that face she gets right before she's about to become apoplectic, when I'm saved by a quiet commotion that ripples through the bar. Heads turn, bow together in whispers and secretive glances, cast toward Gunther's front door.

"What's going on?" my father asks.

My mother leans across the table toward him. "Kerouac," she stage whispers, indicating less unobtrusively than she thinks in the direction of a handsome man who strides in our direction, stopping at a table not far from ours, to chat with some people he obviously knows. My eyes catch his, and I look away. My mother leans conspiratorially closer and says, "Check his feet. I hear he wanders around town barefoot, without any shoes."

"That's what barefoot is, and he has shoes on, Ma," I say, tapping my empty glass that Dad has returned to the table, to let him know I'm waiting on another. "For God's sake, let him be. He doesn't need strangers gawking at him."

Except I am having a hard time not staring myself. He's rather good-looking in person. Dark hair, chiseled cheekbones, if a sort of sad, hollow look in his eyes. There's no doubt it's him. Anyone who lives within a ten-mile radius knows he moved in with his mother a few years ago. To escape from the commercial success of *On the Road*.

I had friends who'd seen him moseying around town, but they don't care like I do. They're not well read. But I've read practically everything he's written. Not just

On the Road three times, but *The Subterraneans,* and I'm right in the middle of *Dharma Bums.*

"My word, he's handsome," my mother says, leaning in again. "Don't you think?"

I do, but I can't bear her fawning, so I ignore her, which isn't exactly fair. She's closer to his age than I am. But only one of us is married. Either way, I'm grateful when the waitress returns with my second drink. I suck on the whiskey-soaked cherries before sipping it quickly down.

I'm sure it's the alcohol that emboldens me. When Kerouac heads to the cigarette machine, I excuse myself from our table, and head in the direction of the ladies room. As I reach him, I stumble. Years later, when I dare tell the story, I'll say "purposely," but likely I catch my heel in the uneven slats of the wood floor. And coupled with the whiskey, well, I stumble right where he stands, and he—Jack Kerouac— catches me, graciously, by the arm.

"You okay, miss?" he asks, and I have to fight to stop myself from swooning.

"Yes. Thanks." Though I've steadied myself, his fingers remain linked around my forearm. His intense brown eyes search mine. Does he think he knows me? Is it some sort of request? Invitation?

"I must have caught my heel on something," I say, giggling. "It's my eighteenth birthday. I've had a drink or two. Legally." I smile on the word "legally," though I'm not sure why. The room spins a little, leaving me glad he still has a hold on me. I glance back toward our table, wondering if my parents are watching, my father ready to spring up to protect me, but the hall curves slightly, leaving us out of view.

"I'm Jack," he says. "And I'm legal, too." His eyes take me in, sending my heart spiraling into the pit of my stomach.

"Ruth," I respond. "And I know who you are. I'm a

reader. A fan. *Dharma Bums* is my absolute favorite so far. I'm reading it right now. Well, not *right* now." I giggle foolishly again. "At home, is what I mean . . ."

"Well, then," he says, and the next thing I know, or at least remember, we've gone out the back door, and I'm pressed up against the building, and Kerouac's lips are on mine, and Bobby Masters is nothing more than a dim memory, some childish fancy, I'll barely remember in twenty years.

"A shithole. I told you."

Max stops the bike at the end of the long gravel driveway surrounded by overgrown yellow-brown grass, and motions at a small house, green paint badly peeling, and two of its four front windows covered in plywood. "You sure you want to do this?" Next to the garage, an old maroon Ford Taurus sits, both its taillights knocked out.

I'm suddenly not sure. Now I get why it's taken him so long to bring me here.

"Don't worry. He's not home," he says, rolling the bike up next to the car. "This piece of shit doesn't run. It used to belong to my mother." I notice the bumper sticker, a faded red-and-white thing with an apple that reads: "Teachers Do It with Class." "I'm only sorry you won't get to meet the old man today," he says, turning off the bike and removing his helmet. "He's a real charmer."

I take off my helmet and hand it to him, and he hangs it from the handle of the bike. As I follow him around the side of the house, and up a flight of dilapidated porch steps through an unlocked side door, he mumbles, "Remember, Jailbait, I warned you."

———

The inside of Max's house is sadder than anything I could have imagined. Water stains on the ceiling, and actual holes in the dirty white walls. The furniture looks like it came from a thrift store, and the worn carpeting smells of mildew, smoke, and stale beer.

As we walk past one of the holes, Max reaches a fisted hand out to it. "For when he gets really mad. God forbid he patch it up after," he says.

"I'm so sorry—" I start, but he shrugs.

"Don't be. Better the Sheetrock than me, right?"

When we pass the empty recliner in the living room, Max kicks it. "And here we have Exhibit A: the Beer King's throne. The good news is, when he runs out of beer at home, and TV shows, he heads out to Healy's for the duration. Especially easy to do when you don't have cable. Basically, haven't seen him since the day before yesterday."

"How does he afford that?"

"Friend of his owns it, so he's got a tab there. He's sort of their mascot, or advertisement, or something—seat at the bar near the window and all that, so the place always looks open for business, and since he can't work a real job on account of his back . . ."

I wait, but he doesn't finish. I do a quick count of the empties on the table next to the chair. Four cans of Budweiser, two bottles of Michelob, and an ashtray filled with cigarette butts, all of which make me wonder if Max also drinks too much, more than he should, more than most kids our age, more than a guy with an alcoholic father should. But I don't dare ask. He didn't want me coming here in the first place.

"What did he used to do?" I ask instead.

"Lineman, electric company. Got hurt on the job six years ago. That's when everything went to shit. The year after, my mom left, and I got held back."

I knew Max had been held back in middle school, but I wasn't sure why. There were rumors, all sorts of dumb stuff, but I learned months ago not to believe what other people had to say about Max Gordon. No one knows him the way I do. They only pretend to. I do the math in my head. Six years ago, Max was thirteen. So his mother left five years ago, when he was fourteen.

"You coming, Jailbait?" He's stopped halfway down the hall.

"Doesn't he work at all?" I ask, catching up.

"Nope, still out on disability. He claims the herniated disks in his neck and his back are stopping him, but I've seen him lift a forty-pound case of Budweisers, no problem. He was probably drunk off his ass when he got hurt in the first place. They pay him something, but I'm not sure what. Enough that they avoided a lawsuit." We stop at a closed bedroom door, and he adds, "A little better in here. You won't catch any diseases, at least," and he turns the handle and pushes it open.

Principal Goldstein marches us single file through the heavy blue double doors and toward the gym. My nerves are humming, and I'm tempted to take your hand, but I don't. We're too old for that. We'll be in high school soon.

"Steven Shilling," you whisper, nodding as we pass a cute boy with shaggy black hair who stands, one leg bent up, leaning against the baby-blue-painted brick wall, talking to a pretty girl with red hair. "He's friends with Ethan's friend Patrick. And Adie McKane. Co-captain of the girls' soccer team."

Principal Goldstein turns and holds a finger to her lips as we enter the gym for the various boring speeches by the faculty and administration.

After, we head toward the C wing where the science classrooms are. You turn to me constantly to mouth things: people you know through Ethan, more gossip. It's all new to me, but you know not only people, but the structure of the school itself, its classrooms and hallways, having been here plenty of times for concerts and honor society inductions and award ceremonies for your star brother, Ethan. No doubt he'll be picked Homecoming King end of senior year.

"Ethan told me," you whisper not softly enough as we

pass room C104, its door bearing a sign that reads: "Never Trust an Atom, They Make Up Everything," "that Kiki Munson smashed it with Max Gordon right in there, after school, behind the high tables in the Bunsen burner lab."

"Who smashed what?" I whisper back, more to seem interested than because I am. I don't know who either of those people are. You cover your mouth to stifle a laugh.

"*It,*" you say, your eyes bulging wide like I'm dumb. "You know, *her. It.* Right there on the floor. The janitor caught them, and Ethan says that Gordon kid tried to bribe him with a twenty-dollar bill. To stay and let them finish up. Like, not even caring what they were doing. Ethan says everyone calls it the Munson Burner Incident. Get it?"

"I doubt that happened," I say. "Did he see it?"

"Well, no. Not him, but his friend Patrick's friend Boris. And he told Patrick, who told Ethan, who told me. But I don't think he'd make that up."

"Whatever. It's dumb," I say, loud enough to cause Principal Goldstein to turn again and sternly pronounce, "Girls, please, quiet. We all need to behave like grown-ups here."

I give you a look, and you say, "Sorry, Principal Goldstein, I'm just trying to show my friend which room is which," and you smile too sweetly, which makes me want to cringe. You seem different today, insincere. Sure, we always share secrets, but this feels show-offy and mean, as if you're trying to prove you're better than me. That you're in on things I don't know about or understand. Besides, I'm sure it's all a stupid rumor, and it's no one's business who does what with whom, even if Ethan says so. And anyway, how many girls would want to go to the back of a science room with him, right? My breath hitches at the thought.

I follow quietly until we reach the freshman biology lab where, speaking of Ethan, he's meeting us, partly because he's Mr. Slattery's favorite, so he's one of the three students walking groups through "Your Typical Day in Bio Lab," and partly because he'll be buddying up with us the rest of the day when we break off into individual schedules—one senior assigned for every new freshman, and you made sure I got to pair up with you.

"Hey, Eth," I say, when we've gathered around his lab table. He smiles at me, eyes crinkling through his safety goggles.

"We wear these for most of our labs," he says, tapping at them. "Chemistry or bio, and there's an emergency sprinkler up there, in case it's needed." He points up to a bronze sprinkler head in the ceiling and adds, "But don't think you won't get detention for setting it off on purpose, and you don't want to end up in detention with the Ellises and the Gordons of the world."

Ethan winks at me, right as the girl next to me leans across to you and says, "I would. At least with Max Gordon. Seriously. Have you *seen* Max Gordon?"

You push her back, and Ethan moves on with his demonstration; everyone, including Mr. Slattery, still laughing, though, for the life of me, I'm not completely sure at what.

If Max's house is sad, his room completely breaks my heart, not because of how neat and clean it is, made up with a green-and-blue plaid blanket and heavy matching curtains on the window, but because of the bookshelves. One whole small wall covered in them.

"Don't laugh, I made those," he says, pointing to the curtains.

"Really?"

"Yeah. I would never lie to you about curtains."

I laugh, and wrap my arms around his waist and bury my nose in his sweet heady scent. "You're seriously going to tell me you sew?"

"Not exactly. Not sew." He shakes me off, and walks over and flips the bottom edge of a panel up toward me and says, "But I can staple pretty well."

I wrap my arms around him again and kiss the back of his neck. More than ever, I want to give myself to him, if not all of me, everything, then at least something big, to make him feel good. "Well, they're nice. It's really nice in here," I offer.

"Don't go overboard."

"I'm not. I'm serious. So, you never told me . . . Does your mom ever come home? Visit, at least? Something?"

It occurs to me how little I really know about him, at least personal stuff like that about his family. Only what he's volunteered, which isn't much. And I want to know everything.

"Nah, she's a little too far for that."

"Wait, where is she again? Japan?"

"Hong Kong."

"Geez." It's hard enough that my father is in California. I don't know how Max deals with her being on another continent.

"Sit," he says. "Enough with the inquisition." He nods at his bed, so I sit, and run a finger along the outline of the squares in his quilt wondering if he makes his bed every morning, or if he just made it today, knowing he was going to ask me over.

"Tell me why she went? I swear I won't ask more after that."

He pulls out the chair from his desk that's across from me, a small wood one, like it's meant for a kid in elementary school, and straddles it, facing me. "She got an offer to teach. They pay well there. And we needed the money. Plus it was a chance to get away from my pops. Enough?"

"But what about you?"

Max shrugs. "What about me? She wanted me to come, and I guess it's pretty much a standing invitation. But when you're fourteen, and all your friends are here, well, Hong Kong isn't the first place you want to split to."

He stands up, walks to his window, and peers out, and for a second I panic, like maybe he's heard a car. But he lets the curtain fall back and says, "Or maybe I felt sorry for the bastard because he was a disabled drunk mess, and couldn't bear to leave him all alone."

"Your dad?"

"Yeah, who else? He's a dick, but it's an illness. And he wasn't always the asshole he is now."

"So, what about California?"

Max sits down again, rests his arms on the back of the chair, and looks hard at me. "What about it?"

"You'll be leaving him soon."

"This is true."

"And?"

"And I guess I've paid my dues. And now I'm going to get us some beers. As for our parents, well, they gotta grow up sometime, right, Jailbait? Spread their wings and fly."

"Mom! Dad! I think they may be hatching!"

It's a Saturday night and Mom and Dad couldn't find a sitter, so they're stuck home watching a movie. "Seriously!" I call, rushing back down the hallway to my room. I don't want to miss anything. I plop myself at my desk and sit motionless like I have so many hours this past week, staring at the big glass bowl Dad bought for me when I said I wanted to raise butterflies at home, like we did in Mrs. Stanley's class.

"You don't even need a kit like she had, or anything," I'd told him. "I watched a video and you can just pick parsley stems and put them in a big jar or bowl with the caterpillars right on them. No food or supplies. They do all the work by themselves."

Dad had found me the perfect bowl, and I'd spent an afternoon parsleyworm hunting in Dad's vegetable garden at the back of our yard. Two days later, at least a few of the caterpillars had attached their heads and tails to the stems like the video showed, and the next morning, like magic, I'd awoken to find those few disappeared inside pale green-brown chrysalises, nearly camouflaged amongst the fading parsley leaves.

Four days more and one of the chrysalises has turned

transparent and is trembling, and Mom and Dad are going to miss it, and I'm starting to get sleepy, so I'm worried I might miss it, too. But I can't sit still, and I don't want to watch it hatch all alone.

I jump up, run to my door, and shout for them to come again. I can hear them in the living room, laughing and talking and probably drinking wine—or, worse, smoking—the volume on whatever movie turned up loud.

Can't they pause it and come?

But it could take hours for all I know, maybe even till tomorrow, before it emerges, and anyway, I don't want them with me if they're going to act all stupid and stoned.

"What's that weird smell? Is that pot?" you had asked one of the first times you slept over.

"Clove cigarettes," I'd lied, and the next morning I'd told Mom and Dad I'd tell all my teachers if they ever did that again while you or any of my other friends were over.

Now I carefully move the bowl to the floor of my room, grab my laptop and pillow and blanket from my bed, and set up camp in front of it. It's not even 10:30 p.m. Maybe if I FaceTime you, you'll stay awake and watch with me.

I call regular first. You answer on the second ring.

"Hey, Aubs," I say. "It's me. Are you sleeping? Turn on FaceTime. Can you? I think the Swallowtails are hatching."

"Really?" You sound confused. Maybe I woke you.

"You were sleeping, weren't you?"

"No, no. It's okay." There's a shuffle of things: you sitting up, your bed squeaking. "Okay, tell me. Right this minute? Tell me everything." Your voice is solid now. You sound excited. I switch the camera on and you're there, smiling. "Is the cocoon thing opening?"

"No, not yet. And it's not a cocoon, Aubs. That's what moths make. It's a chrysalis. And it's not open, but it's turned totally clear and it's shaking."

"Wow, that's so cool." You yawn. "How long will it take?"

"I don't know," I say, honestly. "I'm not sure. It could be five minutes. It could be all night."

"It's okay. Butterfly babies. We should see that together. I'll stay on," you say.

Max returns with a six-pack, and hands one to me.

"Secret stash," he says. "He's too lazy to look for it. It may be warm, but it's way better stuff." I turn the label toward me.

"Max . . ." I don't really drink much, and he knows it.

"What? Come on. It's no big deal. Live a little. We're celebrating." He tips his bottle to his lips and chugs.

"Celebrating what?" The night with Ethan flashes through my mind, the feeling of free-floating, a moth on a carnival ride. I want to be that moth again, instead of the kid strapped in tight, watching, and waiting. I press the bottle to my lips and drink.

"Us. California. The possibilities," Max says. "You being here. Whatever you want."

I swallow sip after sip, my mind spiraling to Ethan. But I force him away. That's a blip. Ancient history. Nothing.

I'm here with Max. And Max is everything.

"Well, look at you," he says, and holds his bottle to mine. I clink it and drink. He polishes his first bottle off before I'm a third through mine, returns it to the empty slot in the carton, and pulls out another and uncaps it. *Salut,* he says, downing that one.

A few more sips and I'm feeling warm and fuzzy inside,

and I don't exactly hate it. So I drink some more, enjoying the feel of my cheeks flushing, and the swirling rush that goes to my head.

My eyes scan the room.

"Who's that?" I point to a poster on the far wall, a black-and-white photo of a black guy with an Afro, a pale purple waft of smoke curling from his mouth. Beneath the poster there's a guitar on a stand, and I suddenly remember Max told me he plays.

I finish the bottle, and lie back on Max's bed. From beneath me, the musky, strong smell of Max wafts up like that smoky curl.

"Hendrix, you mean?" He takes my empty away, and hands me another. I sit up and take a few sips before lying down again.

I close my eyes and imagine him crawling on top of me, pinning my hands over my head, his lips moving down my bare skin as I arch against him. *Ethan* . . . I snap my eyes open.

"Only the greatest guitarist to ever live," Max says. "Please tell me you know who Hendrix is."

"Oh, yeah, him. Hendrix. Right." My words are distant. I feel loose and giddy. I suddenly can't stop smiling.

"Hey, Max, play something for me," I say. "I want to hear you."

"No can do."

"Please." He shakes his head. "I'll make you a deal," I say. I sit up, and locate the bottle, waving it toward him. "I'll finish this, if you play a song for me."

"And what else after that?"

"I don't know," I admit. "We'll see?"

"Fine. Deal. I'll take those chances," he says.

He carries the guitar over and sits back on the edge of the chair. He plays a couple of tunes that I don't know but love, and I close my eyes, letting his voice circle around me, like the butterflies, seeping through me, all warm and raspy and mellow.

The music stops. I open my eyes.

"Pay up, Jailbait," he says.

I awaken at 5:00 a.m. to all my lights on, and you snoring loudly on my phone. We both fell asleep. My battery is almost dead.

My eyes dart to the bowl and I panic. It's not empty, though. Instead, a short, ugly moth-looking thing has broken free of the chrysalis, and hangs there, wet and stubby, not looking much like a creature I'd want to hatch at all.

Maybe they *are* cocoons and not chrysalises.

Alarmed, I hang up, shut my door gently against the early morning quiet of the house, open YouTube, and type in: "Butterfly emerging from chrysalis," then open the first one I come to: "Swallowtail Emerging: Two Minute Time Lapse." It's from the US Fish and Wildlife Foundation, so it should be reliable.

I find my charger and plug in, and watch in amazement as a gross, stubby-winged thing just like the one in my bowl breaks free of its cellophane casing while dramatic music plays. I turn up the volume a little.

"Right after emerging," the woman's voice explains, "the butterfly's abdomen is large and filled with fluid. At first its wings are very small. Over the next several hours, the butterfly pumps fluid from its abdomen into its wings, causing them to inflate."

I watch, sleepy and mesmerized, as the butterfly's abdomen grows smaller, and the full span of its beautiful wings fills the screen.

Later that morning, I walk carefully from my room with the bowl, and set it on the table in our backyard, watching and waiting, all by myself, as the butterfly finally takes off and flies away.

Max unzips his jeans and steers my hand inside. I don't stop him; I help. I want to. I move my fingers down, run them over the surface of his underwear.

"Jesus, Jailbait—" he whispers, as I slip them under the waistband and in.

My fingers touch skin. Max, warm and hard in my hand.

"Don't stop, please," he says.

I don't let myself think, just wrap my fingers and move my hand up and down the way I hope I'm supposed to. He's sweaty, and my hand sticks, and I don't have much room to maneuver. He grows thicker and harder and moves more enthusiastically, bumping my hand against the fly of his jeans. It all feels sort of alien. Not bad, just weird, but nice, too, the way he rocks and moans in rhythm with my hand. As if I'm directing him—conducting him. As if I'm helping him to float away, from his dad and this shithole house, from all the people who don't understand him. He moves faster and faster, and moans some more, and almost as soon as I started, it's done. He grows soft again, and my hand is gooey and warm.

He rolls onto his side, propped on an elbow, and smiles at me.

I'm not sure what to do or say, but he gets up right away,

anyway, so I don't have to worry. He pulls off his T-shirt and tosses it at me. "Here, you can use that. I'm gonna wash up and take a leak," and he disappears into the bathroom.

I lie back on his pillow, my head spinning, and for one split second I think how crazy it will be when I get home and tell Aubrey everything. But that's wrong; that won't happen. She and I are barely friends anymore.

And suddenly I feel like I'm going to cry and I don't know why. Maybe because it hits me that we're really *not* friends anymore. Forget barely. Not at all. And what I wish most in this moment is that I could have her back, the old Aubrey, the one who ran through sprinklers with me, the one who played House and lugged Mary Lennox up on her canopied bed, sharing her deepest, darkest secrets with me. The one who fell into fits of conspiratorial laughter when we caught Ethan looking at porn on his computer. The one I could talk to, who wasn't so different from me.

Lying here in Max's bedroom, I want to feel good about how I'm finally doing in real life all those things Aubrey and I only imagined back then, pretending on hands and dolls, in hopes that one day we'd actually know what we were doing. I miss that Aubrey, the one who would have wanted to know everything about how he felt, and sounded, how it smelled. The one who would have made me spill every lurid detail.

The toilet flushes down the hall.

"You ready?" Max says, walking in and holding out a hand to me.

"Ready for what?"

"Come on, I'll show you. The Kawasaki. My *other* shiny, new baby that's going to take me all the way to California."

He picks me up and tosses me up over his shoulder in a fireman's carry, spanking my butt and sending me into a fit of still-tipsy giggles, even as I fight the rush of alcohol that lurches up from my stomach into my throat.

When he puts me down, we're in the garage and I'm standing in front of a large, gleaming motorcycle, black and cobalt blue, way sturdier and more intimidating than the beaten-up dirt bike he rides to and from school.

"It's the same exact color as a Blue Morpho butterfly!" I say, sounding a little more excited than I should.

"That's what we'll call her," he proclaims proudly. "Blue Morpho. All good bikes have a name." He sits on her and pats the seat behind him. "Hop on. See how she feels. Soon she'll have the power to take me from New York to California in less than a week."

"Us," I say, awkwardly straddling the seat. It's wider than the dirt bike's, and harder for me to get comfortable on.

He twists around to look at me. "Are you serious?"

And maybe it's the beer talking, or that I'm taking Blue Morpho as some sort of big, significant sign, but I meet his gaze and say, "Yes. Completely serious. I have the money, Max. I mean, I think I do. *Could.* And if I do, you can have it." I lean my cheek to his back, wrapping my arms around his waist, pretending we're in motion. I'm safe here with him. I'm happy. He is everything I've waited for. "I want you to have it, Max. All of it. Whatever you need to fix her up. Plus, gas and the other stuff. I want to go to California with you."

He shakes me off and climbs off the bike, stands facing me, hands gripped to my shoulders. His eyes are alive with possibility.

"Are you sure, Jailbait? Really?"

I nod. "Yes. I think so. If the money is still there, it's yours."

If I'm taking Blue Morpho as a sign, I should also take it as a sign that the first Glasswing is dead when I walk in my room. But I don't. It crushes me, but I read nothing into it, just stare at its lifeless body at the bottom of the habitat.

I don't have time for that right now. I have a small window of opportunity. Mom's not home, and the note on the counter says: *At dinner with Nana. Call if you want us to bring you something.* Plus, I'm still slightly buzzed, which emboldens me. I lift the lifeless creature from the habitat and hold it in my palm.

With my eyes closed, it's weightless. I can't even tell that it's there.

It's been months since I've been in Mom's room, months since I've done anything but stand wistfully at her door watching her sleep, or cry, or zone out, or talk to people who aren't there. Like everything else in my life lately, the room feels only vaguely familiar, a set design from some play I once saw.

I sit on the bed, trying to rationalize what I'm about to do. It's not all that hard, actually. If Dad gave a crap about me, I tell myself, he would have come home months ago.

And if my mother cared, she'd snap out of it, pull her shit together. Try harder. Try at all.

The duvet cover is new, expensive-looking cream-colored silk with brown and gold embroidered flowers. I run my hand across it. Leave it to my mother to dine out and shop between crying jags. And this—it feels strangely fussy and old-ladyish. Not like my mother at all. Maybe Nana picked it out. I prefer the old, loud green-and-violet paisley one that, despite a trip or two to the dry cleaners, had still smelled faintly of my father.

I lie back and try to recall the scent, a mix of his cucumber soap and his spicy, musky aftershave, remembering how the smell would engulf me when I'd hide under their comforter at bedtime, hoping to stay snuggled a few minutes more.

Tears well in my eyes. But there's no time for this. I propel myself up, a swell of beer rising in my throat, and walk to the big oak dresser with all the drawers, the top row merely decorative ones that used to fool me into tugging on them before I'd remember they wouldn't open.

I run my fingers across the old photographs spread across the top, and Mom's collection of perfume bottles clustered on an antique silver tray. Some of the bottles, clear glass etched with diamonds and starbursts, others muted shades of oranges and blues, with either those old-fashioned atomizer spritzers attached, or glass stoppers. I pick up my favorite, the periwinkle one with a stopper shaped like the top of the Taj Majal, as if a genie might be secretly captured inside.

The bottles belonged to Dad's grandmother, who died before I was born. As a child, I used to love lining them up across the bedroom rug from big to small, from favorite to least, all the while Mom reminding me to be careful, not to stray from the carpet with them, lest they fall and shatter into a million irreplaceable pieces.

Staring at my old favorite, I realize it's lost its magic. I don't know what I saw in them at all.

Next to the tray of bottles sits a framed photograph of Mom and Dad I snapped right before they left for the Rainbow Room that night. It's shocking how different Mom looked less than two years ago. Her face was rounder, her eyes focused and bright. Don't get me wrong, she's still beautiful, but now her face is thinner, her eyes sunken, her gaze distant and dull.

I put the photograph back and open drawers one by one. They're stuffed to the brim with sweaters and jeans and tie-dyed T-shirts, things I rarely see her wear anymore. I slide my hand around each drawer, under the piles and between the folds, hoping for my fingers to touch metal.

I come up empty, so I return to Mom's side of the bed and search her nightstand, but those drawers hold nothing of consequence either, just old greeting cards, books, and pens.

I lie back, and stare sideways at her nightstand, at the small stack of books there, too. A slim white volume called *On Anarchy;* a pastel-green novel called *Gilead;* a book on Buddhism I've seen her carrying around, with a photo of meditating monks on the cover. And, last but not least, a red-and-white paperback of *On the Road* by Jack Kerouac.

I pick up the Kerouac book and rifle through it. This isn't the one she was reading a few weeks ago; this says *The Original Scroll* under the title. I remember Nana talking about this, how Kerouac had written the book quickly, no editing, on pieces of tracing paper that he taped together into one long single-spaced scroll.

"Imagine the talent!" Nana had exclaimed.

"No, I don't!" I say aloud, and shove the book back, wishing an already-dead author I never met would die all over again.

I walk to the far side of the bed and rummage Dad's night table drawers. There's all sorts of junk in there, too, but nothing resembling the pink metal boxes, so I head to Mom's closet, which is more like a small walk-in dressing room and leads to the master bathroom.

The rods on each side are draped with her silk kimonos. There must be at least twenty in their various Crayola colors, dangling with tassels and ties. Some have belts, others, frog closures of braided rope. She prefers the light skimpy ones that look like lingerie, and flutter against her like a breeze when she moves.

I walk through, arms out, letting the cool fabric slip across my skin, the smell of her, some exotic flower, washing over me.

One of my favorites—blush-pink with dark magenta cherry blossoms embroidered down the front and around the hem—slides from its hanger, so I wrap it around me, and sit at her vanity, staring at my face in the mirror.

My hair is a mess. I gather it in my fingers and braid it loosely down the back. I don't wear much makeup, just eyeliner, the remnants of this morning's now faded brown smudges around my lids. And my freckles, invisible in winter, have begun to dot my cheeks, where they'll come in full force with my tan in summer.

"I like your freckles, Jailbait." I squint, and try to see myself the way Max seems to, sexy and sophisticated like my mother. But all I see is a girl, plain, and simple, and boring, right out of some Norman Rockwell poster. The one with the girl in braids, looking at her reflection in a mirror.

I pull the braid apart, drop my head forward and let my hair fall in front of me, shake it around, and whip my head up, letting it spill wild and full around my face. I pout my lips and put on one of Mom's bright red lipsticks, exaggerating the curves, then find a charcoal eye pencil, and draw myself thick, dramatic lines.

There. Better. I look more like how I feel.

I smile, and think of Max, the sound of him moaning as he moved in my hand. The slick stickiness of him covering my fingers after.

I slip my hands down between my thighs, thinking of how it will feel to have him touch me there, pretending I'm him until I lose myself, my breath fast, then sit, finally, quiet and still.

"There," I say aloud to my face in the mirror. "Better. Now, we have work to do, JL. Money to find. A trip to take with Max Gordon."

I slide open drawer after drawer, wading through miscellaneous pill bottles and old makeup cases and containers, costume jewelry and sparkly hair combs, blow-dryer attachments and brushes, my mother's flat iron, but don't find anything but junk on the left side, or the first two drawers on the right. But in the third drawer down, I feel it immediately, tap my fingernail to metal.

Even without looking, I know.

I pull the box out, and open its dull pink lid, lips dry, blood rushing in my ears. It's just like I remembered: Where index cards might be, a thick roll of hundred-dollar bills.

I slam it closed, slide it to the back of the drawer, and shut that, making sure everything is exactly how I left it.

I turn off the vanity light, needing to think. Sleep on it. If I take it, there's no turning back.

In the bathroom, heart racing, I pee. Only as I flush do I notice Dad's robe on the hook on the back of the door. The pale blue terry-cloth one he wore every morning down to breakfast. I don't know why it surprises me there. I guess I thought he would have taken it with him.

I strip off Mom's kimono, hanging it under some towels on the hook, and slide my arms into the robe, wrapping its thick fuzzy warmth around me, and sit on the edge of the tub and breathe in the soft, distant scent of him.

On my way out, I change my mind again, yank open the drawer with the box, and shove the entire wad of bills into my pocket.

So be it. She'll probably never even notice it's gone.

As I turn to go, I catch my reflection in the edge of the darkened mirror. Red lips, wild hair.

Jailbait.

I smile.

Maybe Aubrey is right. Maybe I'm a slut and a thief and a Jezebel.

I pucker my lips, hold my hand to my mouth, and blow a kiss goodbye to that sweet Norman Rockwell girl.

Part III

Moths, not butterflies, spin silk cocoons.
Butterfly caterpillars molt like reptiles.

LATE MAY
TENTH GRADE

"Jean Louise?" I startle at the light, at my mother standing in the doorway of my room. "Why are you wearing that?" I sit up, my mind racing. *Dad's blue robe.* "Why do you have that lipstick on?"

I wipe drool from my mouth and try to gather myself. *She's not even talking about the robe.*

On my bed is my history book. I meant to wash up, take the robe off and hang it back on her door, and study. My eyes shift to my desk, to the lower left drawer where I shoved the money, wrapped in a wad of construction paper.

"No reason." I shrug, trying to breathe normally. "I just thought maybe . . ."

She walks to my bed and sits. She wears a turquoise kimono embroidered with chartreuse vines.

"You don't need all that." Her voice is dreamlike, her hair wet from a shower. "You're beautiful just as you are."

"Mom!" I stop her. I can't stand it—her—any of it anymore. She has a pile of envelopes in her hand.

I close my history book, push it away, and stare at her.

"Yes?" She lifts her hand from the folds of the kimono, and I can see them, the words, the name, the dreaded purple stamp that's coming in a week or two. A whole new pile. *Return to Sender. No known addressee.*

I turn away, tears stinging my eyes, and yank Dad's robe off and throw it on the floor of my closet, and head to my bathroom to scrub off the makeup. I should have known better than to worry about the robe, about the money, about any of it. I should have known better than to hope for one normal moment with my mother.

"I'm going out," I say, slipping on my sneakers.

"Jean Louise?"

I glare back at her.

"He's dead, Mom! You know that, right? I know you like his books, and Nana kissed him. But he's dead. Jack Kerouac, the author? He's dead. I keep trying to tell you that. Why won't you listen? He died, like a long, long time ago."

She turns to me, a faraway look on her face. "Of course I know that. Don't be silly, Jean Louise."

As if *I* am crazy. As if she doesn't still have the envelopes right there held in her hand.

I know where I'm going, even if I don't realize it at first.

But I'm not sure *why* I'm going to Aubrey's house, or who I'm hoping to find.

The evening is warm; dusk has settled. Max's house, the money, all feel like eons ago.

It's nearly summer. In a few short weeks, it won't turn dark until close to nine.

At the Anderssons' driveway, I stop. Only the red Mustang is out front. The other cars could be in the garage.

Part of me hopes Mrs. Andersson is home. She's not exactly warm, but she's known me forever. Until that stuff with Ethan, she was as close to a surrogate mother as I've ever had.

But that was then and this is now. I'm guessing she knows what happened and hates me for it. Maybe she even told Aubrey and that's why Aubrey isn't my friend anymore. But if Aubrey knew about Ethan, she would have said something to me a long time ago.

There's another possibility: Mrs. Andersson wouldn't have guessed in a million years that Ethan could like me, or put the moves on me, no matter what she might have seen that night. Her precious son would never have done that. I would never have been worthy.

Even if Mrs. Andersson did know, that was nine months ago, and I'm with Max now, and Ethan has moved on to college. Everything is different. And she's a grown-up, so she wouldn't hate me. She would be worried for me. When she sees me, she'll wrap her arms around me and welcome me in.

Don't be such a stranger, JL! she'll say, hugging me. *We don't see you around here nearly enough anymore!*

I walk up the front steps, hope filling my chest, trapped like a cloud in a bottle. Despite me knowing better. I ring the bell and in a matter of seconds, Ethan answers.

He's in shorts, and sneakers, a T-shirt clutched in his hand. Beyond us, his red Wilson tennis bag sits on the hallway chair.

"Hey, Markham!" My heart skips a beat and shadowy thoughts streak through, but if Ethan feels anything but happy to see me, he doesn't let on.

"Did I interrupt something?" My voice shakes. I feel light-headed and stupid remembering how he knows about Max.

"No, just got back from two sets." He wipes his bare chest with the T-shirt. "The 'rents are out to dinner. I was about to shower."

I look away, my cheeks burning. I shouldn't have come here. Not for him. Not for Aubrey. Not for anyone.

I don't know what I was thinking.

"Come in," he says. "Don't just stand there." He smiles like everything is fine and normal.

"Is Aubrey home?"

He holds the door wider, but I stay frozen on the stoop, wondering if there's a way for me to turn around and head back in the direction of home.

"Yeah, she's here. But don't just stand there like a stranger; seriously, come in."

But I feel like a stranger. I pick at a drip of cement on the brickwork that frames the front door, my stomach roiling with hunger, the sour taste of beer rising again. "It's okay. It's nice out. I'm good waiting here, if she'll come down."

He gives me a funny look. "Suit yourself. I'll get her." He heads back inside, toward the center hall stairs, but I call out to stop him.

"Actually, Eth, is she alone?" He turns and studies me, brow furrowed with concern. I wrap my arms tight to my chest and shake my head at him, a plea not to ask questions. I struggle not to let tears erupt. I'm being stupid getting so upset. "It's no big deal if she isn't," I say, sounding utterly unconvincing. "I'm just not so close with her other friends."

He walks back to the door. "You mean Thing One and Thing Two?" he says, lowering his voice conspiratorially, and I feel instantly better, like maybe someone else sees it; it's not only me. Like maybe someone's on my side after all.

I nod and let out a lame little laugh. "That would be them, yes," I say.

"Well, now I get it, and I can't say I blame you. Sometimes I question my sister's judgment. But no, they're not here. Just her. And don't worry, Markham, you guys will be okay." He reaches out and puts a hand on my shoulder and squeezes, sending a surge of adrenaline coursing through me. "Friends go through stuff. Especially girls, you know? You and my sister will be fine. Best friends again in five minutes. Or maybe five days, or five weeks, but you will. So don't let those other girls bother you."

I shrug, wanting to believe him, but I can't seem to find the words to say so.

"Trust me on this, Markham: Once you get out of high school, you won't even care. All this, here"—he motions around him at the front lawn, the house behind him—"is a dim memory. A whole world that's not high school is waiting out there."

"Thanks," I say, trying not to focus on what that makes me.

"Anytime. You sure you're okay, kiddo?"

I back away, enough to cause his hand to drop.

"Yeah, thanks. It's just been a hard few months. I feel much better now."

He squints at the lie. "Well, good, come in. Let me get my dopey sister down here." He takes a step back making room for me, and I follow, but only one step inside the door. "Hey, Aubs, your friend is here!" he yells up the stairs. Then to me, "Hold on, she probably has her music on, and can't hear."

He runs upstairs, and I turn and stare outside, to the stoop, to the front lawn, where Aubrey and I used to have our cartwheel competitions. We would practice for hours, begging Ethan to judge us until we made him crazy, saying he had to score us on all sorts of point scales, legs straight, toes pointed, et cetera. "You're both good," he would whine after the fifth round. "I give you both tens. I'm not playing this stupid game anymore!"

"JL?"

"Hey, yeah." I jam my hands in my pockets and force a smile. I feel like an idiot for being here.

Aubrey stands before me, her curly brown hair piled up with a clip on the top of her head. It looks good like that. Messy. Effortless. I could never do that with my pin-straight hair. I say that, as dumb as it is, and she laughs. "Thanks," she says.

"Anyway, I'm sure you're busy—did Ethan say you had to come down?" My eyes scan for him, but he hasn't returned from upstairs.

"No, not at all. Why? What's up?"

I want to blurt everything, about Max and what I did today, about the money, and how I'm thinking about going to California. Instead, I say, "Not much. I don't know. Nothing really. I just . . . I had a thing with my mom, and one of the butterflies died, and, well, I found myself out walking and . . . here."

She looks down at the tile floor. "Oh," she says, softly. "Do you want to come in and sit or something?"

I shake my head. "Can we sit outside for a few?"

The Anderssons' green sloping lawn gives way to mini gardens that flank each side, perfectly manicured and symmetrical, a tall weeping cherry in the center. When we were little it would drop its pale pink blossoms in profusion in late spring, and we'd gather them by the fistful, tossing them into the air, and watching them fall down on us like magical pink rain.

"Unicorn rain," I say out loud, the name coming back to me.

"Yeah. I was thinking that, too."

"You were?" Aubrey nods. "And remember the cartwheel competitions? How we'd make poor Ethan judge?"

She laughs. "Nothing about Ethan is 'poor.' You of all people should know that." Panic rises in my throat, but she quickly adds, "He's so spoiled, isn't he? Even now, he gets his way with everything. You thought High School Prince Ethan was bad, you should try living up to the U Penn Dean's List King Ethan."

I breathe, relieved none of this is about me. Or me and Ethan. Just about beautiful, perfect Ethan, himself, and Aubrey and me in agreement. And for a while that's enough;

we sit quiet, thinking and staring out at the darkening front yard, the fireflies, appearing, blinking, and disappearing in the indigo air.

"I didn't mean to bother you," I finally say, unable to stand the silence.

"You're not bothering me, JL."

"Well, it feels like I am—like I do."

"Stop. Besides, you're one to talk . . . You're always with *him*." She pauses. "Which is fine, I mean, it's just—*I* tried, remember? Like the time we all—" But she doesn't finish that sentence, either.

I'm not taking the blame for all of this, because once or twice I blew her off to hang with Max. Times when we weren't alone anyway. Those girls were always there.

Anger rises in my chest. I suddenly want her to say it, to tell me how awful I am because I want to spend time with my boyfriend. Because I like *Max Gordon*. Who she thinks she knows anything about, but so doesn't.

"Go ahead. Tell me," I say.

"Tell you what?"

"What it is that's so, so bad about me."

"You're not bad," she says. "Not at all. I feel horrible even saying anything. It's just, it's all weird. It's not like it's even your fault."

"What's not my fault, Aubrey?"

"It's . . . Your mom . . . Well, people talk, JL, and even my parents are worried about you, about us, spending too much time together. They think you're not—They say you're unsupervised. A little wild. You know your parents can be . . . that anything goes in your house—"

"You used to like that," I snap back. "You liked that my parents were cooler than yours. 'Free spirits,' remember? You always wanted to be at my house, not yours."

"I know; I did. I do. But with your mother so, well, maybe it will . . ." Her voice trails off, but I don't need to hear more. The fury is so swift I can't breathe.

"Will what? Rub off on *me*? Jesus, Aubrey! She's sick! She's trying. She's seeing a doctor." My eyes fill with tears, and I can't hold them back, can't swipe at them fast enough as they slide down my cheeks.

"I know. I'm sorry," she says. "You know I don't think that. It's my parents. My mom. She thinks we should take a break. That, with everything going on, maybe that's why you're not like you used to be, and that we—"

But I'm already up and moving toward the street.

"JL! Please. It's just a little break, that's all." I wheel and walk backwards as she moves down the lawn toward me. The lawn where we used to toss unicorn rain and spin cartwheels until we were dizzy. "You're taking this wrong," she says. "Or I said it wrong. They love you, my parents. They care about you. But they think you're acting different, and maybe it's because of the stuff with your mom. It's not your fault. It's *their* fault—*her* fault—that you're behaving like this."

"Behaving?" I stop now and glare at her in disbelief. "Behaving? You're the one who's changed, Aubrey! You're the one who's acting all high-and-mighty with those girls. You're the one judging me."

I start to walk again and she follows me, down to the edge of the street.

"Those girls get straight A's, JL," she says. "Those girls don't drink. Those girls aren't hooking up with Max Gordon."

I whirl around and laugh loudly. I laugh so hard I have to steady myself with my hands on my knees. I'm crying I'm laughing so hard. Finally, I straighten and stare her right in her judgmental face. It helps that I can only half-see her in the blanketing darkness. But I'll be damned if I'm letting her have the last word on Max Gordon.

"For the record, we're not 'hooking up.' And even if we were, we're in love. But you wouldn't know the first thing about that, would you, since you don't have a boyfriend, and never have? And here's another news flash, Aubrey: You don't know the first thing about Max Gordon. You and your rumors and the shit Ethan may have told you years ago, neither of you have any idea who he is. How good he is. Smart and kind and funny. You have no idea what he's been through. So you really ought to shut the hell up."

I don't say more, because I won't have her pity him. I won't betray Max and all the private stuff he's told me. Like he said, he doesn't have anything to prove. And I'm never going to convince Aubrey, or her stupid, judgmental, holier-than-thou family.

"I'm not saying that, JL. But he *has* done stuff. It's not rumors. It's the truth."

"So what?" So what if Max isn't a saint? So what if he drinks a little and gets stoned? This isn't middle school. Half the kids in high school get stoned. Hell, my stupid parents get stoned.

Screw the Anderssons. How do her parents even know about *my* mother? Because whatever Aubrey knows, whatever I've told her, she was sworn to secrecy. I told her in confidence, because I was worried. She promised not to tell.

"People talk," she had said.

What people? Who? Screw them, too. I'm done with everyone. Everyone can go to hell, but Max.

"JL, please—" I shake my head. "You're right. Don't go. Let's talk about this. I—I don't know what to do."

"Forget it, Aubrey!" I call over my shoulder. "No worries. You're off the hook. You and your family are rid of me."

When she calls my name again, I don't even think about turning around.

Mom is still in my room, sitting in front of the habitat, un-moving, as if she is meditating or something.

Does she meditate now?

I have no idea what she's doing.

"Mom?"

"You're back," she says, not turning. "I'm so relieved."

She is?

"Yeah, I went for a walk. Are you—?"

People talk . . . It's not your fault . . . It's . . . Your mom—

"Yes. Yes, of course I am."

"Are you okay? is what I mean, Mom. Not relieved."

Her constant confusion crushes me.

"Yes. I know. And sure. But I'm worried for you. You're my girl. I love you. I want you to be happy." Her words make me uneasy. There's something stilted and off about them, like she's saying them, but they're not quite hers.

I walk over and sit on the floor next to her.

The smell of her still-damp hair, her lotions and per-fume, fills me with this distant, uneasy memory. I'm little, maybe five or six, and we're sitting at her vanity looking in her mirror. She's made room for me on the bench next to her while she puts on her makeup, her jewelry. She picks up a small black bottle with gold letters and holds it out to me in the palm of her hand. The light sparkles off the glass, making it look almost purple.

"This one your father bought for me when we went to Paris," she says. "Hundreds of dollars per ounce. It's made from real jasmine and styrax."

I don't know what either of those things are, but they sound special and rare and exotic. She takes the cap off and puts a tiny dab behind each of my ears, and on the front of my neck. The smell is cloyingly sweet and singes my nostrils.

"According to Cleopatra," my mother says, "jasmine is the scent of seduction. It makes men want you." She puts a dab behind each of her own ears, in the hollow of her throat, and runs her finger down between the crease of her breasts. "Men have always been drawn to women's perfume."

I squirm on the seat, pick up a lipstick, and hold it out, a question. "Go ahead," she says. "You can put it on."

I trace my lips, wondering how she keeps it so neat and perfect when she does it. Not that she wears makeup much. Only when she and Dad are going somewhere special.

"Legend has it, Cleopatra coated the sails of her boat with her perfume as she was returning to shore, in order to lure Marc Antony to her." She leans in to me and whispers this next part as if it's some sort of secret between us. "It worked for your father." But the cloying smell of the perfume still makes me want to gag.

Now she squeezes my hand, her slim fingers over my own. "I've been sitting here, the whole time you were gone, watching them," she says. "They're so beautiful. I don't know why I haven't come in to see them sooner. These are the ones Nana picked out, yes? These clear ones?"

"Yes." I'm surprised she remembers, that she's been paying attention at all. Maybe she's not as bad off as I think—as bad off as Aubrey and her family believe.

People talk, JL . . .

Maybe she's really okay, or the medicines are starting to do their job.

She moves closer and runs her fingers down the mesh of the habitat. "Tell me again what they're called."

I swallow hard, mad at myself for nearly falling for it, this trick where she acts like everything is fine, like she's better. I've seen it before. It's a trap—this mother who seems present, who asks questions. This mom who seems halfway normal. This version of her is way more dangerous.

"JL?"

"Glasswings," I answer. I stand up, to gain some distance. "Those clear ones are the Glasswings, and the grayish-white ones are Painted Jezebels." I sit on my bed and open my history book. Anything not to let my heart believe what she's saying. "There were four of those to start, but one died earlier. I flushed it down the toilet."

I'm being purposefully harsh and callous. That's not what I did. I carried it out to the garden.

On the end of my bed is the small stack of envelopes she walked in with. A reminder of what she is, and is not: her endless letters to a dead man.

I gather them up and bury them at the bottom of my wastebasket.

"The Glasswings are from Central America. Nana picked them," I say, only to distract her from what I've done. "They feed on nightshade plants, then store the toxins, so prey can't eat them."

"They're so beautiful," she says. "So fragile. I'm amazed you know how to take care of them." I let my eyes go to her as she pushes up from the floor, and moves toward me, reaching her arms out. I let her do it, embrace me. I can't help it. This day has been long and exhausting. I don't have the energy to ignore her. "My precious, precious girl," she whispers into my hair, "you're growing up so fast. If I'm not careful, I'm going to miss it all."

I tense against her chest, even as I feel my resolve melting. Her soapy smell winning me over. The sweet, slippery promise of her love.

"We should do this more," she says, stroking my hair. "Spend time together, take advantage of it being just us girls."

"I'd like that," I whisper.

"Your father will be home soon."

I push away and look at her funny. Has she spoken to him? I thought it was early September now. Four more months, he had said. But I'm guessing it's only her wishful thinking. Her believing what she wants to believe.

"I'm trying," she says. "You know that. I know I've been depressed. But I'm feeling much better. Dr. Marsdan says it's a matter of finding the right combination of things."

"I know." The cloud of hope fills my chest once more. "We can let them out if you want," I say, nodding to the habitat.

She claps her hands together, and sits on the floor again, and I walk over and pull the mesh flap aside and relocate an orange slice from a perch to the outside top of the habitat. Almost immediately, a few butterflies emerge.

"That's a Jezebel," I say, pointing. "They fly higher than the Glasswings. Closer to the ceiling. It's instinctual, because their food sources are high up in the trees." My mother's eyes follow, big with childlike wonder.

I tap on the mesh where the Jezebel whose wing I repaired stays safely inside. "And this one, here," I say, showing her, "she had a broken wing, and I fixed it."

"No kidding?"

"Made a splint out of cardboard. I watched a video," I explain.

"Well, that is completely remarkable," my mother says.

I kneel next to her, and she turns and tucks a strand of hair off my face. "Do you know how truly special you are? You are so much more than I will ever be, Jean Louise. Beautiful and special."

"I am not," I say. "All my friends always say how pretty you are. That you look like a movie star. They think you're my sister. Max can't take his eyes off of you."

She shakes her head. "Don't say that," she says.

"It's true."

"Jean Louise, please, that's terrible . . ."

Anger rises in my throat. Is she serious? Does she think me saying it aloud is the problem? Maybe if she wouldn't walk around half-naked.

"Come here. Please. Let's don't." She pats her lap, and I give in, sitting against her, like I would when I was little. I rest my head back and look up at her. *We're both messes, aren't we?* She wraps her arms around me, as the butterflies circle above.

I close my eyes, and think of how it would be to fall asleep like this, listening to her breath, to her heartbeat, to her voice sharing hushed promises—promises I know, even at not-yet-sixteen, she can't keep.

I slide my tray along the metal rail staring at today's gourmet choices: sloppy joes made with gray chopped meat that looks like it's been sitting there all weekend, heaped onto a half-stale bun, or "Tacos Fresco," which is the same gray meat slathered in cheese and sprinkled with lettuce, plopped in a half-stale taco shell.

My stomach roils as I move past the rectangles of main course offerings, fingering the wad of bills in my pocket that I was crazy enough to bring to school. I twist and search for Max in the crush of kids. I wouldn't have even come to lunch except for the plan to meet him. But he's not here yet. He rarely comes to lunch anymore.

When we first started dating, I used to sit with him and Bo and Dean and their girlfriends, Angie and Melissa, which was super-uncomfortable, but at least I had someone to sit with, not to mention Meghan and Niccole were equally uncomfortable to be with. At least Angie and Melissa weren't fake, if they didn't seem all that interested in having some sophomore hanging out with them. But by spring, they'd all become mostly absent from the premises, plagued by serious senioritis.

"What are you having, dear?" The lunch lady's voice is impatient. I twist back to her, apologetically, and order.

"I'll have two side salads." She gives me an exasperated look. "Sorry. Not that hungry," I say.

"I'll have to charge you full," she says, and I nod, then walk with my tray of wilted lettuce and two mealy tomatoes, looking for somewhere unhostile to sit. Across the cafeteria, I spot Meghan and Niccole by the door, so I stay put at the opposite end of the lunchroom.

I wonder where Aubrey is. Maybe she and those girls had a falling-out. But so what if they did? Screw Aubrey.

People talk, JL . . .

I don't need her. I need to stop thinking I do.

At a table against the windowed wall, I spot Tanya and Janee, the girls Aubrey and I used to hang out with in middle school. They're giggling with Matt Chin and Steven Piscarello, possibly two of the geekiest guys in school.

I steer past them, to the last table, and sit down opposite some stoner girl I don't know but think may be friends with Bo's girlfriend. She doesn't look up or say hello. But she doesn't tell me to leave her alone, either.

"Hey," I say, forking lettuce unenthusiastically into my mouth. Her eyes lift and she nods. I guess she isn't much in the mood for conversation. Fine with me. I'm just biding my time till Max gets here.

I manage to finish the first salad in peace before there's a tap on my shoulder. I turn to see Aubrey standing there, her face knotted with concern.

"Hey," she says, her eyes darting to the girl across from me. "Mind if I sit down?" I finger the lump in my pocket, eyes searching for Max.

"Sure, but I was getting ready to go."

She doesn't have food or a tray, and when I glance back to where Meghan and Niccole were sitting, they're gone, so maybe I was right. My chest flutters with momentary hope.

"I only need a minute." The stoner girl casts us a look,

picks up her tray, and leaves. "Sorry, it's a free country," Aubrey mutters.

I fork at my second salad, before pushing it away. "So talk," I say.

"JL . . . I—Please. I feel bad enough."

"So don't."

"Come on." She reaches down and touches my knee, but I move it.

"Don't want you catching anything slutty," I say. It's completely juvenile, but I can't help myself. Hurt has settled like a dead bird, all weight and wings and bones in my throat.

"We've always been friends. And you're not perfect." I glare at her, and she shakes her head. "Sorry, that's not what I meant. I—I want us to be okay." I flinch, and she sees it. "Or, not that, I guess, because, of course we are. We will be. I wanted to know that *you're* okay."

"So nice of you. I'm fine. Thanks for checking."

"That's it then?" But I don't answer. I don't have one. She's trying, but what am I supposed to say after she basically told me her mother said she should stay away from me? And, anyway, I don't have time for this. Max is making his way across the cafeteria.

"JL?" Aubrey waits, following my gaze. "Oh, sorry," she says. "Never mind. I guess, I'll get going."

"Sure," I say, standing. I need to head off Max saying anything that might hint at what I've done. What I'm *doing*. What I brought here for him. "I'm sorry, Aubs, I should go."

"No worries. I get it," she says. "I just wanted to try—I mean, to invite you—that's why I came over here. We're going to study for finals together at my house, if you want to join. You're welcome to. I mean, we want you to." But I barely register her words because Max is across the room faster than I can extricate myself from Aubrey or the table.

"Hey." He nods at her. It's not enthusiastic, but at least it's polite. "You ready? Let's get out of here, Jailbait," he says.

"Okay, coming."

"Don't bother," Aubrey says, standing. "I'll go."

"Suit yourself, Andersson."

"Max—" I try, but it doesn't matter. She's up and leaving. A few steps away, she stops and turns, arms crossed to her chest, voice shaking.

"For what it's worth, JL? You shouldn't be so hard on Meghan and Niccole. They know you don't like them. And that makes it hard for me. And I'm trying here, so maybe you could try a little harder, too?"

Such a lie. Why can't she see they have it in for me?

"Sure," I say, trying to swallow past the dead thing in my throat. "I will."

"Okay, see you later," she says, and she's gone.

"What was that about?" Max asks, sitting. I can barely look at him, barely talk, even though I'm desperately happy to see him. I want to fall into him, have him wrap his arms tight around me. I want school to be over. I want summer to be here. I want everything to be easier. I want to be sixteen, headed to California on the back of his bike.

Three weeks till my birthday. Three weeks till the end of school.

"Jailbait? What happened?"

"Nothing." I shake off the question. I don't want to focus on any of that bullshit. "Hold out your hand. Under the table." I shouldn't do this here, but I do. I pull out the wad of bills and slip it in his hand, closing his fingers around it. "There's two there," I say, my voice lowered. "That should be enough to fix Blue Morpho?"

He stares down and shoves the wad of bills into his pocket.

"Hundred?" he whispers. I shake my head. "Thousand?" I nod. His eyes grow big, concerned. "Jesus, are you sure, Jailbait?" I nod again. "No way. I can't. Seriously."

But I hold my finger to his lips and look him in the eyes.

"I want you to. Really. And I want you to take me with you."

I pull Dad's blue fluffy robe from my closet, and wrap it around me like a cocoon. Mom hasn't said anything about me taking it or wearing it around the house like pajamas. It makes me feel close to him. It makes me believe he's coming home.

I lock my door, and slide my desk dresser drawer open, and unwrap the rest of the wad of bills, the empty pink box still in Mom's vanity.

Twenty bills gone. Fifty left.

Seven thousand dollars altogether.

How much had Max said we'd need? The stack I gave him should be enough for Blue Morpho.

I count the bills into stacks of ten, to be sure. Five stacks remain, the bills crisp and untouched, if curled from being rolled up so long.

My heart pounds in my ears. I've given Max two thousand dollars. What if I shouldn't have given him so much?

But, no. Max loves me. He must if he's asked me to go with him.

"Come on, Jailbait, we're going for a ride." Max walks over to the broken garage door and yanks it up, letting sunlight pour in. When he returns, he grabs two helmets down from a shelf, holds one out to me, and stands proudly in front of Blue Morpho. "Voila. Hop on."

I stand there confused. "Already? How'd you fix her so fast?"

"Not fixed yet. Waiting for parts. But we're not going far. She'll be a little bumpy, but she can weather a short ride with my girl." He takes the helmet from my hand and straps it on my head, wrestling a bit to tighten it. "Adorable," he says, touching my nose.

I smile but can't keep my nerves from showing. I'm barely comfortable on the dirt bike, but if I plan to ride this thing to California with him, I had better get used to it.

"Oh, and other than me," he says, as I climb on the seat behind him, "you'll be the first one on her, and that's special, that's *sacred,* so I wanted you to know." I smile again. I know how he feels about these things. "Wait till you see where I'm taking you."

He turns the key in the ignition, stomps once, twice, three times, on the starter thing, and jerks us forward out into the sunlight.

And we're in motion.

This is Max and I trust him, I tell myself, trying to stop my arms, wrapped around his waist, from quaking.

I trust him.

Otherwise, I won't be able to keep my grip and hold on.

I trust him.

As he zips down the side streets and onto Main, weaving in and out of cars and buses, as I cling to him for dear life. Petrified that, despite the small comfort of the helmet, I'm going to fly off the back at 60 miles per hour and break every bone in my body.

I trust Max, who hangs a left at the end of the road and flies past the Hay & Feed.

I trust Max, who signals at the exit ramp and turns onto the freaking turnpike.

I trust Max, who thankfully veers us off at the New Waverly exit, and aims us in the direction of the abandoned New Waverly Mall, a site suspended mid-construction going on two years.

The stores are in various stages of half completion, some sections merely framed, others nearly finished, the main billboard at the turnpike exit that used to announce: "Waverly Mall, Where All Your Shopping Dreams Come True!" changed by some vandal to announce: "Waverly Hell, Where All Your Shopping Dreams Come to Die!" Under that, they've added: "Shoppers Repent! In the Name of the Father, the Son, and Abercrombie & Fitch!"

The rear of the construction site is a notorious hangout for derelicts and bikers and homeless people, so I hope to God that's not where we're going.

"Max!" I yell, tugging his shoulder as he slows off the highway, and eases us into the cracked and overgrown parking lot. He calls back, "Don't worry, it's fine. We're not staying here. Promise!"

"I trust Max," I whisper, as he heads beyond the south side of the site where a "Macy's Coming Soon" sign still clings to the blacked-out windows.

When we reach the back, he says, "You ready? This is the part where you really need to hang on," and he takes off flying, my head jerking back, barely giving me enough time.

He shows off like a little kid, making wide circles, zig-zagging the bike around the raised bumps intended to slow traffic down. "You'd better hold tighter than that!" he yells, heading us beyond the lot, toward the acres of undeveloped land.

I close my eyes and clutch to him as hard as I can, whispering, "I trust Max," for the tenth time, even as I'm having a hard time knowing if I do. Even as the back of his leather jacket proves nearly too stiff and slippery to hold on to.

He doesn't slow down and turn to check on me until we've reached the edge of a badly overgrown field. "Okay, here we go," he says, and he moves the bike forward on the soft dirt, the stalks of green growing taller, grazing at my ankles, the sides of my bare legs.

Halfway out, he stops. "And now, the magic!" he yells over the bike's engine. "Watch how everything changes!" He plows forward, slowly, till the green starts popping with color: reds and blues and yellows and purples, as far as the eye can see. We're in the middle of a vast wildflower meadow, right on the cusp of the woods. He cuts the engine altogether, and I scan the width of the field, taking in daisies and buttercups, violets, and dandelions. "The blue ones are called Bachelor's Buttons," he says, "I did an image search on my phone."

"And these?" I extend my flip-flopped toes toward a patch of fuchsia flowers with jagged edges.

"No idea." He laughs.

"Well, it's beautiful."

"You like?" he says, turning back to me.

I nod. "I do, Max. It's breathtaking. How did you know this was here?"

"Happened upon it," he answers, which makes no sense since we're off in the middle of nowhere. "I figured it was a good place. I wanted to thank you. And ask you something."

My heart ramps up. Something about the way he asks. Maybe he wants me to sleep with him now. And maybe I want to. Maybe I will.

"Take your helmet off," he says. He lifts his off and straps them both over the handle.

I run my hands through my hair, damp with sweat, from fear or heat I'm not sure. Loosed beads trickle down my neck and into my shirt. I gather my hair into a fisted ponytail, but I have no elastic, so I let it fall back. I shift my jaw, sore from the stress of clenching my teeth the whole ride here.

I wait for us to get off the bike, but Max doesn't, so I stay sitting, rest my cheek against the warmth of his leather jacket.

"Nice, right?" he asks. "Peaceful. Quiet. I can feel your heart beating."

I close my eyes. "You can?"

"Yeah, I like it."

I smile. *What if I really do love Max Gordon?*

"So, can I ask you something? A favor?"

My heart starts up again. "Sure."

"Can I touch you? Just like this. Not looking, or anything. Just sitting here, like this." He moves his hand back, behind him, and rubs my bare leg.

"Yes," I say, even though I'm not exactly certain what he means. I just know that I want him to.

"You sure?"

I nod once more against his leather jacket as his fingers move inward, tracing their way between my thighs. Down to where the seat of the bike meets my skin. Slipping inside the loose, willing hem of my shorts.

"Just one," he says, letting his thumb find its way in under the fabric, onto the outside of my underpants.

My heart ramps up so hard, he must feel it, and my breath comes in short bursts; the sound of everything all but disappears.

I want this. I want Max to touch me; I want to feel the way I made him feel.

His thumb circles—softly, gently for a while—then slips in under the wet cotton edge of my underpants.

"You feel so nice," he whispers.

I take shallow breaths, feeling him there, my body quivering and electric, as if he's plugged me into a socket. I try to relax into it, to him, my cheek against warm leather, his thumb on me, pressing softly, nothing between us, skin to skin. Moving in small, perfect circles.

And then I go light-headed, and I swear my heart flutters and stops, and my arms rise up and I fly away.

EARLY JUNE
TENTH GRADE

The next day Max invites me to prom.

We're sitting on the wall after school, and Max Gordon asks me, Jean Louise Markham, to go to *prom*.

"What the hell are you talking about?" I ask, my eyes practically bugging out of my head. "You hate school. You hate convention. You hate prom."

He laughs. "All true. So, will you?"

"Will I what?"

He laughs again, shakes his head, rakes his fingers through his hair, and kicks a small piece of cement out from between the low, large stones of the wall with his boot heel. It lands with a melodic little *thunk*.

Max Gordon is uneasy. Uncomfortable. I turn and squint at him.

"You heard me, Jailbait. I asked if you want to go to prom."

"Seriously, though? I didn't think you were serious."

"Well, I am. Dead serious. No prompsal, though, that shit is stupid. Consider yesterday in the field my promposal." I punch his arm. "What? Wasn't it good?"

My cheeks redden. "It was," I say, embarrassed that just the thought of it sends a rush between my legs. "But why do you want to go?"

He jumps down off the wall, and kicks the landed cement lump across the sidewalk into the parking lot.

"Why not?"

I jump down, too. I need to see his face. I'm pretty sure he's putting me on.

"Um, because you're Max Gordon, and only a few short weeks ago you called prom something super obscure and poetic like 'conformist bullshit geared at the pathetic, lemming-like masses'?"

He grins and says, "Yeah, I can be a dick, so I probably said that."

"Also, you said you hoped those pathetic masses might, to quote you, 'hurry up and wither and die.' Or was that some line from a sonnet?"

Max throws his head back and laughs fully now. "You're a trip, Jailbait, you know that?" I shift my eyes up to his. "Come here," he says, pulling me in and hugging me. He kisses my hair, breathes me in. "You should know better than to listen to me. On anything. I just say stuff to sound subversive. Besides, I don't know, with graduation coming, maybe I'm feeling a bit nostalgic."

"Seriously? You?"

"Yeah. Why not me?"

"I don't know, Max. Why not?" I give him a suspicious look.

"Or, okay, let's suppose that a few of us got together and talked about things, and decided our prom-going can, and should, be a contrary political statement. Like a message to all those jocks and other assholes that they don't own the freaking school. That prom isn't theirs, graduation isn't theirs, and they don't own them any more than Christians own reindeers and fir trees just because they've commandeered them for their totally merchandized holiday."

"Ohh-kay," I say, having no idea what he's talking about

anymore, but it doesn't matter because he picks me up, and places me on the wall again.

"So you'll come?" He wedges himself between my legs and looks up at me with big puppy-dog eyes. "Plus, I want to show you off," he adds. "Show everyone how beautiful you are."

I roll my eyes, but he gives me this look, and suddenly I realize he's not joking. Maybe I underestimate how much Max likes me.

But prom? With him and his friends I'm nothing like, who barely tolerate me?

"Yes or no, Jailbait?" he says.

"Yes. Of course, Max. Yes," I say, even though it doesn't give me a whole lot of time to find a dress and shoes and I've never even mentioned to Mom or Dad or Nana how old Max is.

"You're the best," he says. He buries his head in my chest and turns it side to side, before slipping down toward the vee of my legs on the hot wall. As if he's going to try to do something here, in broad daylight.

"Max, stop."

"What?"

"Max."

"Nobody's here but us, Jailbait."

"I'm serious."

He stops, stands up, gives me a wounded look. "Okay, fine. But if you think my hand is good, wait till you feel my tongue." I roll my eyes and jump down, but his words and meaning are already sending a thrill racing through me.

We walk to his dirt bike, and he hands me my helmet. "We want you to be safe," he says.

"Shut up, Max."

He laughs. "Oh, okay. And not only that," he says, climbing on. "But, you should know, I can't wait to fuck you. I want to fuck you so bad." He pats the seat behind him and I get on. "Come on, genius," he says, twisting around to smile at me. "I'll take you home so you can study, and be good."

June unfolds. Two more butterflies die. Amazingly, the Jezebel whose wing I repaired remains.

Mom continues to slog off to Dr. Marsdan, and Nana continues to act like everything is normal and okay.

Nothing stops the Kerouac letters from flowing.

At least Dad hasn't called to delay again, which means he's still slated home by the end of August, or maybe early September.

Fine by me. I'm happy he'll be there all summer. He's my excuse to head across country with Max.

Dad, my abandoner and my alibi.

Finally, something to thank him for.

"Hey, Dad, it's JL. Guess what?" I've been practicing aloud when I'm alone, working on keeping my voice steady, my tone nonchalant. I've been working on a script: *As soon as school ends, I'll fly out,* I'll tell him. *Spend the whole summer there with you.* Then I'll have Mom or Nana drop me at the airport here. And Max will meet me there an hour later on Blue Morpho.

Sure, there are still kinks in the developing plan. Time discrepancies. The fact that Dad will want to buy the tickets and it'll take days, not hours, to get there with Max. Either I lie to Dad about flights, or I lie to Mom about flights, and convince them to let me order the tickets myself. I'll have to do some maneuvering and hope they don't talk with each other, trusting me, instead, with the details.

It will work in my favor that Mom doesn't have a firm grip on reality anymore.

And, once I'm there, I'll finesse seeing Max. Or admit to Dad that part of the reason I wanted to visit him was that Max is moving there.

Sure, it's complicated, and there are too many moving parts. But it's not like anyone is paying me too much attention over here.

I close and lock my bedroom door, put on Dad's robe, and walk to my desk, sliding open the bottom drawer. Unfold the purple wrapper like magic origami.

The remaining bundle is smaller, only forty bills, since Max needed some more for stuff he was working on.

"You don't have to," he'd said, but I wanted to.

I peel five more bills from the pile, fold it back inside its paper, and wedge it to the back of the drawer. One week till prom, and I really need to go to the mall.

I need a dress. And to tell Mom.

Add it all to the growing list of things causing me panic. Prom, sandwiched between my US History and chem exams. Two subjects I've been slacking on. Two subjects I usually study with Aubrey for. The administration does this on purpose: puts prom in the middle of finals to discourage overnight plans, or too much partying.

To discourage underclassman like me from attending.

They didn't used to, but then some dumb tenth grader got so drunk a few years ago he had to go to the hospital to have his stomach pumped. I'm sure his date was thrilled.

I haven't told Max yet how I need to be home right after.

I figure he knows, and I'll feel like a baby having to tell him. But there's no way I can stay out all night. Even if I didn't have tests. My average has taken a dive in both those classes. I need A's or I'm going to suffer a big slide.

I turn on my computer and search "prom dresses that make you look cool," but even before I get the word "cool" typed in, "skinny" and "thinner" come up, cool not even being a pre-searched option. I sigh, and search by color, instead, but everything seems too frilly and ridiculous, or too slutty, which would make Aubrey and everyone else happy.

I shut the computer, and walk to the habitat. The Jezebel whose wing I fixed lies motionless in the corner.

No matter how hard you try, there's no saving anything in the end.

My chest squeezes at the thought. And at the one that follows: *The rest are going to be dead soon, too.*

I pluck her out, and rest her in my palm, touching her where the splint I made so many weeks ago is embedded in her wing, then wrap her gently in a tissue and head out back to bury her in the garden.

When I come inside, Nana and Mom have arrived home, their hands full of shopping bags. Macy's. West Elm. L'Occitane. I wish I had known they were going to the mall.

"Jean Louise!" Nana drops her bags on the table, and throws her arms around me. "Your mother and I have gone on a bit of a spree. We got some pretty things for you, too, of course. Now, if I could only figure out which bags."

She walks back to the table, rummages through some of the bigger bags, producing a small paper bag from a store I like called Trinkets.

"Probably too much bling for you, I'm guessing. That's what they call it, right? Bling?"

I nod, suddenly overwhelmed with guilt, for stealing, for plotting to leave with my boyfriend, for everything. It would break Nana's heart. She may not ever know about the money, but she'll be crushed if she finds out I've lied, that I've gotten on a motorcycle and headed off to California.

Then again, isn't she always going on about Kerouac? He was more than twice her age when she kissed him. But that was only a kiss. She didn't flee cross-country on his motorcycle.

"You only live once, right?" she's saying. "You'll see why I couldn't resist."

Mom is quiet, busying herself at the sink with a glass of water, and the arrangement of various pills. She counts, tapping her finger, loses count, and starts over again.

"Lottie!" Nana calls to her. "Where's the other one? The bag from Bloomie's?"

Mom doesn't answer. She's propped against the sink, staring down into it at something. Did a pill go down? It can't be the dishes. She hasn't made a home-cooked dinner in weeks.

"Plus, it's almost summer, and you do have that sweet darling boyfriend . . ." Nana chatters on, oblivious, not seeming to notice my mother, or how she hasn't given her an answer. I don't understand her. Does she think it is normal for Mom to disappear like this in a matter of minutes? Just because she's also capable of going shopping? Not to mention, she's called Max darling, which makes me want to laugh. Only clueless Nana would call Max Gordon darling.

"Jean Louise," she says, "come here and see!"

I open the Bloomingdale's bag absentmindedly, pulling a soft, wrapped object out and placing it on the table. I unroll it from the paper and a black bikini with purple and orange butterflies spills out.

"They're exotics, just like ours!" Nana says. "Butterflies

for our butterfly. We want you to feel pretty while you're lounging out around here this summer. Right, Lottie?"

My mother still doesn't answer.

The dead Jezebel wrapped in tissue.

The pink box of money.

Me, on Max's bike, his thumb moving in small delirious circles.

"Max asked me to prom," I blurt, pushing the bathing suit aside and waiting for some sort of reaction. Mom stays bent over the sink like she's going to puke. Nana says, "Well, isn't that lovely?"

"It's next Thursday."

"Wonderful!"

Wonderful? That's it?

All that worry for nothing. Do they even realize what this means? That I'm barely sixteen, and dating a boy who is about to graduate? A boy who plans to have sex with me in a hotel room halfway between here and California?

"Do you like it?" Nana asks, nodding down at the bikini.

"Yes. Thank you. It's beautiful."

"Go on, open the other one." She hands me the Trinkets bag. "This is where the blingy part comes in." She giggles a little. Mom pulls a wineglass down, retrieves a bottle from the fridge, and heads off toward her bedroom.

Nana's eyes follow her, and she turns back to me with a tight smile. "Well, go on," she says, pushing the bag toward me.

"Nana, should she be drinking? With all that medication?"

"I'm sure it will be fine," Nana says.

"But . . ."

"No worries, my pet. Open your gift. I know your mother. Everything will settle when your father gets home." I take a deep breath in, and pull out a pale pink folded square. "It's a T-shirt!" she says, stating the obvious. I shake it out in front of me.

A bird in flight, outlined in rhinestones, graces the front. And on the back, the words *Thursday's child has far to go.*

"It's from the nursery rhyme, about the days we are born? You've heard it, yes? 'Monday's child is fair of face, Tuesday's child is full of grace. Wednesday's child is full of woe, and Thursday's child has far to go.' And so on. And you, my child, were born on a Thursday." She strokes my hair. "So true, isn't it? You have your whole life in front of you, and far to go."

My mind races, wanting to take it as a sign.

"You don't like it?" Nana asks. "It's too blingy, isn't it? I thought—"

"No! No, Nana." I try to think of the right words to say. "It's just what I needed. It's perfect."

"Well, we can always return it if you don't like it. It was in the window and I thought it was calling your name. How I remember that night, so long ago, waiting for you to arrive. And your mother—she was in such a state, worried about everything, as if she was the first woman in the world ever to give birth. Poor thing was exhausted, had gone into labor the evening before. I had to leave our weekly bridge game to meet your parents at the hospital. More than thirteen hours later, four o'clock Thursday morning, you finally decided to arrive! How you kept us all waiting in anticipation!"

I lay the shirt on the table and trace the rhinestoned bird with my finger, then flip it over to read the words again:

Thursday's child has far to go.

I am going, aren't I?

Maybe I should give Nana a chance, first. Tell her everything. Let her see that something has to be done about

Mom. Something more than she's doing already. Tell her about the talking to no one, calling Max "Jackie"—about the letters. How can she not be seeing these things?

But how can she help if the doctors aren't helping?

"I love it," I say, instead. "Thank you."

Her face brightens. "Well, that's wonderful, isn't it? I'm two for two! And here I am going on and on when I'm sure you have studying to do. So, as long as everything is under control here . . ."—she looks around at our neat house and makes whatever assumptions she needs to—"I'd best get home."

I shut my door and open the habitat so the few remaining butterflies can come out if they want. I shove the new bikini in my drawer, and pull on the T-shirt and stare at myself in the mirror.

Goodbye, butterflies. Hello, sparkly bird.

Nana is right. Thursday's child has somewhere far, far away to go.

Part IV

Several types of butterflies have false eyes to scare off predators. Humans are not so lucky.

I come home from school the next day to a black garment
bag on my bed, a folded note on top written on Mom's sta-
tionery, in her fancy script:

My darling JL,

*I know I've not been much use lately, but a girl going to
prom needs a dress.*

Will this work?

I love you,
Mom

*P.S. Please invite Max over for dinner beforehand.
Nana and I would like to get to know him better and
take pictures.*

Tears spring to my eyes. I've been too hard on her, thinking she's not paying attention when she is.

I unzip the bag, and pull the dress out, a simple one-
shouldered, floor-length chiffon sheath, totally plain except

for a high, thin moss-green belt. But what's most amazing is the color: cobalt blue, the same exact color as Blue Morpho.

I hold the dress to my body and twirl in my closet mirror, blown away by how perfect it is. The fabric is weightless and sheer, nearly iridescent, like butterfly wings.

I strip off my clothes and slip the dress over my head. It glides down my body like a waterfall, cascading to the perfect length on the floor. I look pretty, even if it doesn't transform me completely, into something beautiful and rare like my mother.

I twirl again, faster and faster, the fabric billowing outward, and lift my arms, moving across the floor, as if waltzing with an invisible partner.

When I return to the mirror, I stare at my cheeks, warm and flushed, my chest heaving, my hair a mess, wisps fallen across my cheeks in slashes. I want to call Aubrey and show her how perfect it is.

Instead, I call Max.

"Come see," I say. "I think you'll love it."

I just want him to be okay with the dress.

"Hey, what happened to them all?" he asks when he walks in my room. He runs his fingers down the mesh of the habitat.

"They died." My tone may be matter-of-fact, but I'm crushed about it.

"That's sad," he says. "I guess they really don't live very long."

"Some of the more common ones live less than a week. But I used to let those out, so I'd never see them die." I laugh a little because I don't want things to turn morbid. Not with Max here. "Tropicals live longer than most. Maybe I'll set the rest of them free this weekend."

"Still sucks," he says, turning back to me. "So, put it on." I tilt my head in question, and he says, "The dress, Jailbait? You wanted me to see."

"Oh, not on, just . . . well, here." I slide the hanger out, press the dress against my body. It looks like little more than a slinky blue sheet hanging there. "It is way better on," I say quickly.

"I bet," Max says. "So, go ahead."

I glance at my door, at the hall. Max stays put. "Can you wait out there?"

He furrows his brow. "No. I want to watch you," he says.

My face flushes hot. "You want to see me put the dress on?"

"Yeah. Can I?" I lay the dress on my bed and wrap my arms to my chest, self-conscious. We've done all sorts of things together, Max and me, but it's not like I've paraded around naked.

"Okay," I say, tentatively. I close my bedroom door. Who knows when Mom might return? Swiftly, I pull my T-shirt off and toss it on my pillow, leaving on my white bra with black polka dots and black bow. A breeze from I don't even know where slips across my stomach, raising goose bumps on my skin. I unzip my shorts and let them fall to the floor, but don't turn around, leaning over my bed to slip on the dress.

"Wait, don't. I want to see you completely."

"Max . . ."

"Please? I won't touch. I just want to look at you." I turn to face him, my arms hanging awkwardly at my sides. I swear I can feel my entire body blushing.

"Same as a bikini, you know," he says, and he's right, so why does it feel so different? "God, you're gorgeous." He moves toward me. "Can I take this off?" Without waiting he reaches around and unhooks my bra. I can feel my heart pounding right out of my rib cage. "I want to see all of you in daylight."

He takes the straps from my arms, tosses the little piece of fabric onto my bed, and says, "I want to know you, Jailbait. I want to touch you, taste you, all of it."

He cups my breasts and kisses them, making goose bumps rise up everywhere now, and kneels in front of me, running his tongue down my stomach and over the front of my underpants.

"Max—" I whisper. The truth is it's hard to say no.

"What?" He looks up at me, but doesn't move, instead pulls the edge of my underpants aside, and slips his fingers under. "It's okay to like it," he says. I make a weird, out-of-body sort of noise, and he starts to move his face down, but I reach and hold it by the chin.

"We can't, Max. Not here. Not now."

"It would only take a second."

People talk, JL . . .

A Jezebel is a whore. And it's just kind of odd that, of all the butterflies you could have picked—

"Soon," I whisper, "I promise," and he shakes his head, but pulls his fingers back, and gives me a swift kiss on the outside of my underpants instead.

"You shouldn't worry about what other people think," he says, standing. "You should only care what you want." He moves to the habitat and turns his back to me. "Okay, I'm not looking. Put the dress on."

He's frustrated. Annoyed. And I feel bad. I want to give him what he wants.

And he's not wrong: What *I* want, too.

He tugs at the Velcro flap as I slip the fabric over my head and buckle the velvet belt. "Hey, can we let them out?" he asks.

"Sure." I turn to face him. "You can look now. It's not special," I say. "Or fancy. It's just, well, the color."

He turns, and smiles, adjusting the crotch of his jeans. "Oh, it's special. It's perfect. Like you. And, therefore, apt to kill me."

"Max, is it?"

"Totally. Classy, or something, like a model would wear. Or a movie star." I snort, but he says, "I never dated a girl like you, Jailbait. You're like every kind of good thing there is. But I'm not gonna lie. It's getting harder and harder to keep waiting."

"I know," I say. "That's why I want to go with you to California. I can't . . . I need to get out of here."

"So, you're really serious?"

What did he think? The money was just for him? I walk to my desk, the fabric swishing between my bare thighs, pull open the bottom drawer, and fish out the rest.

"Super-serious," I say, unfolding the purple sheet of paper and holding it out to him like a gift. "As in, I've never been so serious about anything."

His eyes grow big. "What's that for?"

"Us," I say. "You, if you need it. Or want it. I don't even care, Max, as long as we're together. As long as you take me with you."

"Are you kidding me?" He takes half the bills, returning the rest to the paper. "I can't take all of it. No way." He shoves what he took into his pocket. "And this dress, and you in it?" He picks me up and swings me around. "The most beautiful thing I ever saw my whole fucking life on this planet."

When I walk into my house after school, the air holds that eerie kind of quiet that makes the hair on my arms stand on end. The kind that is often met by my mother whirling through rooms in conversation with no one. Or with her wrapped under covers for days.

With a stack of letters waiting to be mailed to a dead man.

The living room is empty.

"Hey, Mom! You home?"

In the kitchen, I stop and freeze.

She's standing, quiet, at the kitchen sink, barefoot, in a cherry-red kimono.

Her back is to me, shoulders hunched, head down, so at first I'm sure she's crying. And next to her: one pink metal box, lid open.

I suck air.

She knows.

She's going to kill me.

I search for a quick lie, something that, once shaped, might turn into a feasible explanation.

For why I found the money and took it.

For why I was looking in the first place.

Nothing comes, and then: *A school trip.* Or a bigger lie: *Dad called and asked me to look for it.*

"Mom?"

She whirls around, eyes strange and far off.

Well, screw it. She's a mess. Maybe it's time for the truth.

After all, I'm not the one who has gone completely off the deep end. I'm the one suffering, trying to get through. I'm the one paying the price.

I'll tell her the truth. That I'm leaving. Until Dad comes back, I'm going to live with him. Going with Max. Staying for the summer, maybe longer. Until she gets real help. Gets better. Until one of her cocktails kicks in.

"Jean Louise!"

My legs shake. I feel like they're going to buckle right under me. I ball my fists, ready to confess.

Wait—she's smiling?

"I'm sorry. You know I'm not much of a baker, so I was concentrating. Plus, look at this chicken scratch!" She waves an index card at me. "It's impossible to make out my mother's handwriting. I'm so glad you're home! You can help me."

And now I see the snow down the front of her red kimono. The white smears that dust her cheeks, the delicate flecks of dandruff in her hair.

Flour.

I see the bag, too—King Arthur's Unbleached—sitting open next to her on the counter.

The lump of dough.

The rolling pin.

Berries. And a pie tin.

My mother is baking.

Or trying to.

My eyes shift back to the pink metal box. The index cards in it.

It must be a different one.

I take a few steps closer.

Recipes.

A recipe box.

She doesn't know about the money.

I nearly collapse from relief. I nearly start laughing. And really, my mother is so off, so out of it, even if the money was missing, she might not even know. She might think she spent it herself. Bought some stamps. For her nine thousand letters to Jack Kerouac.

"Why are you baking?" I ask.

"I'm making a pie; I told you," she says cheerfully. "Come help." She turns back to the lump and starts kneading.

My eyes shift again to the pink metal box as I walk over. She's propped the index card up against the coffeemaker. At the top it reads: "Nana's Famous Loganberry Tarts."

"That's for tarts," I say, pointing.

"Tarts, pie, all the same," she says.

In the sink is a strainer full of blueberries, their empty plastic containers rinsed and stacked to the side.

"I don't think those are loganberries, either?" I say. She laughs, and blows a wisp of hair from her eyes. I reach out and push it behind her ear for her, slip an elastic band from my wrist, and pull it into a ponytail. "You're supposed to tie your hair back when you cook."

"Hard to find those," she says.

"Elastic bands?"

"No, silly." She rubs her floured cheek against her shoulder. "Loganberries, Jean Louise. Loganberries."

She has the lump of dough flatter, starts to work at it with the rolling pin.

"Where did you think you could get them?"

"Damned if I know," she says.

I stand watching, confused, yet a little elated. She may be acting weird, but it's been months since I've seen her look this happy. She rocks with the roll of the pin, singing some weird tune I've never heard of:

"Your lips are sweet as honey,
Red as loganberry pie.
I could pinch your cheeks like dough.
You're the apple of my eye."

My mother is baking and singing. My mother doesn't cook, let alone bake, so my head spins, trying to understand.

"And why exactly are you doing this?" I finally ask, reaching into the sink to grab a handful of blueberries. I toss them in my mouth, and add with a mumble, "Making pie?"

"Because I spoke to your father, and we're celebrating." My heart skips a beat. *Real spoke or fake spoke?* "He's coming home, Jean Louise! First week of July, possibly sooner." I nearly choke on the berries. "Home for good. Once and for all! Isn't that wonderful? Something that calls for pie, don't you think?"

"Tarts," I snap, angry. Furious. I can't think straight, I can't deal with her, and I sure don't know what to believe. Has Dad really called to say he's coming home or is it some wishful, delusional hallucination? And, if he is coming home, what will I do about Max? Now that Blue Morpho will be fixed, he can leave. How will I lose him after everything?

I race through the alibis I've spent sleepless nights perfecting, the phone calls I've rehearsed, the intricate stories. If I can't go, and he's leaving in two measly weeks, I may never see Max Gordon again!

I cough on the lump of blueberries, mingled with tears lodged in my throat. I can't let them spill. How will I explain tears in the face of her very good news? News I've been waiting more than a year for. Already she's staring at me, waiting for me to join in her jubilation.

I need time to think. What if it is the end of June? That would still give me a week after school ends to make the trip with Max, and have a few days alone with him, before flying back home with my father. I can tell Dad I want to see Malibu before he leaves, how I'm sorry I haven't come sooner. How I'll help him pack up his things.

That way, I'll have a little more time with Max, and get my father back home. I'll worry about the rest as it comes.

I look at my mother, but she's returned to her mess, to pressing and pinching piecrust into the tin.

"Your lips are sweet as honey,
Red as loganberry pie.
I could live forever on your sweetness,
If you'd only let me try."

My mother is celebrating. Singing. Making loganberry pie without one real loganberry in sight and I'm even considering what she's saying might be the truth? When there's not one good reason to believe her.

I walk around her to the other side of the sink and pick up the box, identical to the one I took the money from. I remember at least two more like this, from the morning after the Rainbow Room.

"Where are these from?" I ask, picking through the recipe cards with my finger.

Mom turns. "Oh, those are Nana's recipes. She wrote them all in duplicate by hand when I got married."

"No, the boxes," I clarify.

"Oh, those? Why?"

She turns back and looks out the window, gazing over our pristine backyard, and sighs. I feel it in my bones, the grave shift in her mood, the fall from whatever high she was on to some catastrophic low. I wait for the shoe to drop, but all she says is, "Did you know, Jean Louise, that it's impossible to find actual loganberries? I tried. I went to three different markets and called two others, but decided these other berries would have to do."

"Blueberries," I say, because it shouldn't be that hard to call them what they are.

"Yes, of course. Blueberries." Her voice is laden with sorrow, and when she turns back to me, she studies me like she hasn't seen me in days or maybe weeks. "I was planning to make two pies. One for us to celebrate, and one for tomorrow night, for that handsome boyfriend of yours."

Prom.

Shit. Tomorrow night.

I forgot to thank her for the dress.

"The dress, Mom, thank you. It's beautiful."

Her eyes dart up. We've both lost our grip on what we're talking about.

"It's your birthday soon, right? Sixteen. Imagine that. A girl needs a beautiful dress."

I swallow hard. I wasn't even thinking about my birthday. Because of where it falls, we usually celebrate it the first week of summer, once school ends. But other than a cake and some presents, I'm getting too old for parties and plans. "We'll get you something new, as well. And when your father comes home, we'll all celebrate."

"Okay," I say, holding out the box. "But, Mom, I asked about these. What are they from? Are they Nana's?"

"Oh, those?" she asks, surprised. "No, why?"

"No reason. Just interested."

A wistful smile spreads across her face. "They were mine from when I was little. Nearly antiques, now, I guess."

"Stop it," I say. "You're not old."

"I am," she says. She holds her hands out in front of her, then drops them to her sides. "I can't even look at my hands."

I shake my head, and slide the box in front of her. We both know that she looks way younger than she is. Which is already way younger than most of my friends' parents. She and Dad married junior year of college when she found out she was having me "by surprise." Surprise being code for "not a mistake because we love you, but not exactly using a reliable form of birth control, either."

"Nana saved them," she says, picking up the box and inspecting it before pushing it against the backsplash under the window and tapping the lid back down. "She saved all my things. These were in a box of stuff she packed up for me when she and your pop-pop moved to the smaller house off Main Street, and we bought this one. They were originally a set of six. I don't know what happened to some of them. I think I have four left. They're for treasures." She smiles, her thoughts far off, and I wonder briefly if she's thinking about the money. God forbid I've made her want to look for it.

"I remember," she says, brightening. She motions me over and we sit at the kitchen table. I study her as she talks. As always, she seems so normal on the surface. Just someone's mother. *My* mother. The way she always was. But that's never been the case. She's not like other mothers, and never has been.

"We got them for school, eighth-grade English, I think

it was. I had this teacher, Mrs. Marcaras—but we called her Mrs. Maracas as in 'shake your maracas,' you know?" She shimmies her chest at me and chuckles, which brings me back to all the things I hate about her. For starters, her half-dressed self in one of her endless dumb kimonos.

You should put something on, I think about demanding, *stop wearing those dumb things even when company is over.* But this whole moment is teetering on something dangerous and I don't want to be the one to set her off.

"Anyway," she says, "Mrs. Marcaras made us take all our notes on index cards the entire year, and keep them in order in boxes. All numbered. For the whole entire school year. And everyone else had these ugly green or gray plastic boxes, but leave it to Nana to find me a pretty, pearly set of pink. I remember how pleased she was that day." She shakes her head, her hair splaying about her shoulders, specks of flour scattered in it like the finest powdered snow. "So, I saved them. Used them for knickknacks and such, all these years . . ."

Her voice trails off and I hope she won't add more, but she does, sitting up taller as if the memory has surfaced out of nowhere. "Money," she says. "All that stupid bonus money your father left me. I shoved it in there, hid the boxes away." She laughs. "I didn't want it, JL, did you know that? I'm not even sure I remember where they are."

My chest squeezes tight. I get up and walk to the fridge, pour myself a glass of juice, and offer her one, but she shakes her head, and gets up, and walks back to the sink. She runs the water, squeezes soap in, drops the bowls, and utensils, and rolling pin into the sink. Chunks of flour cake together, float on the surface like mini icebergs. I stand beside her and watch them as they bounce on waves created by the movement of the dishes.

"You're sure Dad's coming home? This month?" I finally brave the words, and it's only when I say them directly, out loud, that I feel the deep longing in my chest, the hope and excitement at the prospect of my father coming home to us for good. Like I used to feel in the early days when he'd visit.

I wait for her to answer. When she doesn't, I turn to her.

"Mom," I say more forcefully, "are you sure he's coming home?"

"What?" Her expression has fallen, as if an unseen eraser has passed over the face of the woman who was standing there a minute ago.

"Dad. Coming home. End of June. First week in July, latest."

"Did I say that?" she asks.

"Um, yeah." I drop my empty glass in the sink, a rage moving up through me, erupting sour, bitter, in the back of my throat. The smell of burning sugar wafts from the oven; the sound of something sizzling emanates from within.

Mom looks back at me, her face confused, her eyes blank, yet filled with fear. She wrings her hands. "Oh, yes, that's right," she says. "Your father called me, right? He told me. I remember."

And I know.

I slip an oven mitt from the drawer and move toward the oven, but she takes it from me, and pulls out the pie herself.

"Shit, shit!" she whispers, dropping it hard on the counter as if she's somehow managed to burn herself.

She tosses the mitt in the drawer, and stands forlornly

in front of the not-loganberry not-a-tart pie, its edges half-burnt, her eyes filled with tears.

"The truth is," she says, shoving the pie into the water-filled sink, and watching it disappear under the dirty, soapy water, "I really have no idea."

I slip the blue sheath over my head, adjust the belt, and stand in front of the mirror, pulling my hair up into a messy sort of cascading bun. I put on gold ballet flats, and small gold heart earrings, and stare at myself in the mirror.

I wish Aubrey were here. I wish she were going with me. I wish she could tell me whether to do the belt higher or lower, whether to leave my hair down or up like this.

A brief flutter ripples in my chest, and a smile spreads on my lips, because maybe she knows and she's jealous. But it fades as quickly, and a wave of dread washes over me. Aubrey and I were supposed to go through this together.

The bell rings promptly at 6:00 p.m. I slip off the dress, and pull on shorts and a T-shirt. I don't need to get a stain on it before we leave.

By the time I get out there, my mother has answered it. Good news: She's not in a kimono. Less good news: She's in a low-cut black cocktail dress that might be the same one she wore the night of the Rainbow Room. She holds a pair of strappy black heels in her hand.

For a split second, I think about going to my room to

change back into my dress, but that will only make things worse. Who can compete with my mother?

Max wears a dark gray suit with a black shirt and—my breath catches—a cobalt-blue pocket square, with shiny black shoes that I'm guessing he bought with the money I gave him. I don't mind. He looks amazing.

"Well, don't you look handsome!" Mom exclaims, opening the door wide for him. I don't think I've ever seen Max in anything but jeans, a T-shirt, and work boots, so he seems a little stiff as he walks in. Hot as heck, but uncomfortable.

"Mrs. Markham," he says, "these are for you." He holds out cellophane-wrapped flowers. Red roses with white baby's breath.

She drops her shoes on the floor to take them and says, "Aren't you the charmer? My word," then moves toward the kitchen, calling, "Let me get some water for these!"

I give Max a shy peck on the cheek, and he hands me a plastic container with two white roses and a blue flower of some sort in between. "That's for you. I think the blue one is an orchid. It goes on your wrist."

"Thank you, Max. It's beautiful."

"I wanted blue for the dress, but white for you. 'A cream-white rosebud/With a flush on its petal tips;/For the love that is purest and sweetest/Has a kiss of desire on the lips.'" He bows deeply and says, "Courtesy John Boyle O'Reilly."

"Who?"

He laughs, but leave it to Max to be reciting some sonnet I've never heard of. When he straightens, he gives me a once-over and says, "So, you decided on wearing that?"

I laugh now. "No, goofball, I just didn't want to get anything on my dress. I'll change after dinner. Come on." I pull his arm and lead him into the living room, and we sit awkwardly on the couch, the dumb Kerouac book staring up at us from the table. I get up, and carry it to the audio cabinet and shove it away.

"What are you doing, Jailbait? You know I love Kerouac," he says, as Mom returns, carting hors d'oeuvres that clearly came from the freezer section of Costco, but that she has presented on a fancy white ceramic platter of Nana's we use only on good occasions. As if she's slaved over them. She places it on the coffee table and sits on the other side of Max, and spends the next several minutes fawning over him, and regaling him with pointless stories about her college days before she met Dad, like anyone cares. Once, she gets up and sashays back into the kitchen in her slinky dress and bare feet, for more food.

Anytime Max—who is clearly dazzled—says anything the slightest bit funny, she tosses her head back and laughs like it's the most brilliant, hilarious thing in the world. The whole display reeks of crazy, not that Max seems to care.

"You didn't tell me how smart he is, Jean Louise."

"I did, actually," I say, cringing at her use of my first and middle name. "Mom, where's Nana?"

"She was running late. Said something about a stomachache." Mom frowns, and I wonder if she remembered to invite her. But none of this is the worst of it, because when we move to the dining room for dinner, Mom pours us all wine in her fancy crystal glasses, quickly refilling Max's, which he finishes off in barely three sips, even though I remind her we're both underage.

"You can't always be so careful, Jean Louise," she says, dismissing me with some ass-backward wave of her hand. "Sometimes, you have to live a little. In Europe, kids drink wine at dinner every night, even when they're ten, twelve years old."

Max raises his eyebrows, and smiles. As if he agrees, but

also like he's starting to realize my mother is at least teetering near, if not slipped off into, the deep end.

"Well, funny that, we're not in Europe, Mother," I say, sounding as snarky and petulant as I feel. But she simply waves me off with another flick of her hand.

"Red wine is good for you. It keeps you young."

"Well, you sure don't need that, Mrs. Markham." Max holds his glass up to her. She looks away, embarrassed, insisting simultaneously that Max call her Charlotte, causing me to wish I were, *in fact,* either dead or *in* Europe.

"Why, thank you, Max! Speaking of living a little, did Jean Louise tell you how my mother once dated Jack Kerouac?"

"Not dated," I mumble. "Just kissed."

Max sits up. "No, that's incredible!"

"I'll get the food. You tell him the story, Jean Louise." She disappears into the kitchen.

"Jesus. She didn't *actually* date him," I say.

"A passing fling, really!" my mother calls from the kitchen, exaggerating. "He lived near here for a time, way back when. Did you know it?"

"I'm not sure," Max says. "Yeah, maybe I did hear that."

"It's true," she says, returning with a large tray in her hand. "Same town I grew up in. Right around the corner from my mother."

Dinner is a prepared roasted chicken from Delaney's, the gourmet deli around the corner, plus some mashed potatoes I assume also came from there, or maybe a box of instant. All on another fancy serving dish as part of some greater ruse.

"Tell me more about this shared love for Kerouac we have," Mom says, not helping my lack of appetite. I have to force myself to stay at the table. But maybe I'm being ungrateful. I should be happy she cared enough to have Max over for dinner, and Max seems to be enjoying it, wolfing it down with relish.

"You know," he says, looking up, mouth still full, "I read a lot. My mother made me when I was little, and my father doesn't, not at all, so . . . Anyway—" He forks in another bite and says, "I read somewhere that the whole wrote-it-in-three-weeks story isn't exactly true."

"Wrote what?" I ask, taking another sip of wine. I may not know what he's talking about, but I'm getting better at this whole drinking thing. Half a glass and the room isn't even spinning yet.

"On the Road," Max says. "Legend has it he wrote the whole thing in three weeks on one continuous scroll."

"Oh right," I say, remembering. "The scroll thing." I take another sip of wine and try not to roll my eyes.

Mom looks up, concerned. "It's true, isn't it?"

"The scroll part, yes," Max clarifies, "but not the three-week part. He'd worked on it for months, writing pieces in notebooks. You might say he *typed* it in three weeks." He finishes his glass of wine and pushes back his plate. "Thank you, Mrs. Markham. This was delicious."

She smiles at him. "You should get ready, Jean Louise. It's probably time for you two lovebirds to go."

Now I do roll my eyes, but I'm happy to be done. I leave Max at the sink handing dishes to her, and go to my room to change into the blue chiffon gown. Ten more minutes and I'll be out of here. Away from this house and my new mother, the crazy Amanda Wingfield version. And only a few days more till I'm on the road with my boyfriend. The real road, not some dumb novel I never read and don't really care about at all.

The limo honks. I take one last glance in the mirror, say a small prayer, and head outside.

WINTER
SIXTH GRADE

"No, JL, you hold it like this." You pour another splash of grape juice into your mom's crystal wineglass and pick it up by the stem with your pinky out.

"Aubs, I think that pinky thing is for tea," I say, but you shake your head and insist, so I copy you, lifting my "wine" to my lips. "Okay, fine, like this?" I ask.

"Yes, and you have to sip slowly, or you get plastered. Like my mother was last Thanksgiving. That's what my dad called her. *Plastered.*"

"Really?" I ask, and you nod, holding a finger to your lips as Ethan walks through the basement with a laundry basket in his hand, plowing through the center of our fake restaurant we've set up. We've named it JL Aubrey's because that's how clever we are.

"What are you goofballs doing, besides trying to break Mom's good glasses and burn down the house?" He nods at our table we've covered with a fancy lace tablecloth. In the center sit two lit candles in pretty silver candlesticks, the bottle of Welch's grape juice we swiped and wrapped with a taped-on sheet of construction paper where you've written *Aujean's Fine Wine,* a bit more clever, at least, by virtue of being a mixture of our first names. We each have a plate of tuna fish and Cheez Doodles in front of us.

"Put on some clothes, Ethan; you're gross," you say, ignoring him. You're good at that, but I'm not, especially when he's parading around the house in his boxers, his body slim, but also kind of built from a year of working out to try to make varsity tennis. I blush a deep red as he shakes his head at us and heads off into the living room. I pray you don't notice.

"Anyway," you say, leaning into me, once he's disappeared into the laundry room, "she puked all over our cousin's living room rug, and my father didn't talk to her for like a week."

"Really?" I ask again, distracted. Even if you don't care what he thinks of us, of all these silly games we play, I do. I want to close up shop and go upstairs and watch Ethan get ready for the ninth-grade dance, see him all dressed up in his suit and tie.

"Really," you answer, as Ethan emerges, the top half of him covered in a white button-down he must have gotten from the cedar closet. He's carrying a blue suit on a hanger as he heads past us toward the stairs. "He thinks he's so great," you say, loud enough for him to hear, "just because he's taking Ashley Mathers to the dance."

"Well, I heard my mother tell her friend that she and Dad ate these special mushrooms once, and they made her hallucinate that she was attending the royal wedding. And when she woke up the next morning, she had cut up the curtains and made them into a dress. Anyway, I've had real booze lots of times," I add, because I want Ethan to know I'm not some baby who only plays pretend. "Just a few sips, though. It's not a big deal if you have a little."

"Have not," you say.

"Have too."

"Prove it, Markham," Ethan pipes up. He hangs the suit on the banister, walks around us, ducking behind the basement bar, and fishes out a bottle full of clear liquid.

He pours some into my grape juice and says, "Go ahead. No big deal, right?"

"Ethan!" You cover your mouth and shake your head, but I'm not about to let Ethan make me look like a liar, so I pick up the glass and swig it down. Ten minutes later I'm in the bathroom puking it up and Ethan is crouching beside me with a hand on my shoulder.

"Remember this, kid, so you don't brag about doing dumb things when you're older." He hands me a wash-cloth. "It's not cool to be like that, okay?"

Half an hour later, he's dressed in his gorgeous blue suit, his blond hair slicked back with a little bit too much gel, and Ashley Mathers is at the door in her pretty purple dress, her parents next to her, ready to drive them to the school.

"Promise me," I tell you that night, when we're curled up for sleep, you in your bed, and me on the floor in my sleeping bag we keep at your house for when I crash here. "Promise me we won't be losers, that we'll have dates for the ninth-grade dance, that we'll wear pretty dresses, and we'll go together."

"I promise."

"No, get the list," I say, tapping your night table drawer where I know your journal is.

You switch on the light, and pull it out.

"And add 'Don't drink too much, or show off,'" I say. "'Or puke our brains out because some dumb boy dares us to.'"

The minute I see the limo, I know I've made a cosmic mistake. I don't know why I thought it was a good idea to go to senior prom with Max and his friends.

That I could handle it.

That I wouldn't feel like some out-of-place loser.

The only saving grace is I still feel the wine coursing through my system. Otherwise, I'm pretty sure I'd turn around.

But I don't. Won't. Max holds tight to my arm and says, "Look at me, getting into this motherfucking fancy shit with the most beautiful girl in the universe," so I'm pretty much getting inside.

The windows are open and Dean and Bo and Angie and Melissa are all laughing loudly, the pungent smell of skunk drifting out. Max steers me to where the driver stands holding the back door open. I'm surprised he's letting them smoke in the car.

"Hello, miss," the driver says, waving me in. Close up, he's younger than I thought.

"Wait, Jean Louise! Jean Louise!" My mother is running down the driveway in her slinky dress, waving her cell phone in her hand. I can feel the eyes of the two girls burning through me. "I promised Nana I'd get photos! I need to get photos before you go!"

If I've despised my clueless pathetic mother more than in this moment, I can't remember when.

Max says, "Sure, Mrs. Markham," and I stand stiffly next to him, trying to smile, while my mother moves her cell phone around, pressing spots on the screen.

"Oh, shoot, hold on, hold on, I've got it." She giggles drunkenly, and I wonder only vaguely if I should invite the others—why not?—in all their stoned glory, to join in.

When we pull away from the curb, I relax a little. I still feel awkward, but a certain giddy excitement kicks up as the chatter sets in.

The seats in the back of the limo face each other with some legroom in between. A mini bar is built into the door on the far side. Fancy crystal tumblers sit in cup holders, filled with some brown liquid that threatens to slosh over the sides with each turn.

Bo passes the joint to Max, who inhales deeply, and raises his eyebrows at me. I shake my head and look pointedly at the glass divider, then back to him.

He exhales. "Don't worry. Dean's brother owns the company. That's Pete up there. Right, Pete?" Pete waves into the rearview mirror. "We have permission to have a good time as long as we don't bust anything up."

"Or puke!" Pete calls.

"Or puke in here," Max echoes.

Angie, whose short black hair is dotted with rhinestoned skull barrettes tonight, laughs, forcefully blowing out a drag she'd been holding in, and taps my knee, the fabric of my blue dress, with a combat-booted foot, and says, "I don't really like this shit, either. How about a drink instead?" She smiles at Melissa, whose hair used to be a solid shade of magenta but is now blue with white-blond chunks running through.

"Yeah, same," Melissa chimes in, and I realize they're both wearing combat boots with their dresses, one of which isn't a dress but a floor-length skirt with a T-shirt and black leather bomber jacket. It looks cool, and I feel silly and out of place in my gown and ballet flats.

"I mean, I'll take a hit or two sometimes, but I'd rather have a rum and Coke." She passes one of the tumblers to Melissa, and one to me. "Go slow. They're more rum than Coke, and your boyfriend here says we need to go easy on you."

"Damn straight," Max says, throwing an arm around me.

I sip the drink down and lean back against the seat, closing my eyes as my body warms to the alcohol, and let the sounds and smells of the car begin to waffle around me. Spaces open, places for me to sink in and breathe, as if I belong.

"Here goes nothing, *chicos* and *chicas!*" Max shouts suddenly. My eyes snap open. The driver has eased us past the ornate gates of the planetarium, tires crunching over gravel as he pulls into a parking spot and unlocks the doors. Max holds up his glass, and the rest of us raise ours, clinking glass to glass, and polishing off whatever liquid remains. *"Veni, vidi, vici!"* he toasts.

"We come, we see, we conquer!" Dean yells.

"Here come the fucking Proletariats," they all chime in, Max closing with, "One last time to live it up big!"

SUMMER
BEFORE FOURTH GRADE

"Here we are, Pippi!" Dad pulls open the car door and tugs on my pigtail, and I slide out and take his hand. "Milky Way, here we come!"

Here is the Hager Planetarium, Mom's and my favorite place in the world.

Mom adjusts her hat, checking her reflection in the window, before we head toward the hill that leads to the main building together, her long gossamer skirt floating up like a breeze, Dad's giant size 12 Birkenstock sandals making their clomping swish-swash noises on the uneven cobblestone path.

"I'm not a Pippi," I pronounce suddenly. "She has braids and red hair and freckles." I want to be something prettier, like Mom.

"Hmmm, how about a butterfly? Le Papillon?" He says that last part with a flourish of his hand.

"Who's that?"

"Not who. A what. It's how you say 'butterfly' in French."

"Yes, okay, that," I say, smiling.

Halfway down the hill, Mom lets go of Dad's hand and skips ahead, stopping to twirl under a cherry blossom tree releasing its last remaining pink petals, arms out, head back, hair flying out like a butterfly. The way I want to be.

"What a perfect day!" she says, clapping her hands together when she stops. "All this, and stars and planets, too!"

Dad laughs and calls, "And which constellation are you, Charlotte?"

"Hmmm. How about, Cassiopeia, the Queen?"

"Too weighty," Dad says, catching up. "I know. Apus, how 'bout? Bird of Paradise. Never with two feet on the ground."

Mom laughs and takes his hand. Maybe I want to be that instead. A Bird of Paradise.

No, papillons *sound so much prettier,* I think as we make our way down to the cool, quiet insides of the planetarium.

The show is my favorite: *One World, One Sky.* It starts with a sunrise over a neighborhood that looks and sounds like ours, with birds chirping and children playing in yards, and dogs barking, and parents leaving for work. But when the sky grows larger and the Earth smaller, as the camera pans out wider, the yards change so there are chickens and oxen and dry desert sand, and when they zoom in again, it's clear they're not in our country anymore, but in China or Africa or India.

"We are all one world, when the stars come out," the narrator says, as daylight fades, and the whole entire room fills with twinkling stars and constellations, and you'd bet a million dollars you were floating outside in the night sky.

When the show ends and the lights come on, Dad gets up, but Mom sits there, unmoving. Her cheeks are wet, and her eyes are glossy with tears.

"Charlotte, really? Now?" Dad asks, impatiently, but I get it, how the stars like that, all swirling and infinite and dizzying, can make a person feel like they need to cry.

Back out in the daylight, we make our way through the rose garden labyrinth, and Mom's mood improves. She stops every few steps to scoop handfuls of peach and lemon-yellow and magenta petals that have fallen to the ground.

At the stone wall that blocks us and the land from spilling down the cliffside into the Sound, Mom reaches over, Dad holding fast to the back of her blouse, to pick some sort of tall, stiff grass with a feathery bit on its end. It looks like wheat stalks, only greener. She threads the rose petals onto the stalks, and ties them into circles that she places like fairy crowns on our heads.

Toward the back of the property, we move past the small building where the mummy is housed—Dad knows I won't go in there—to the reptile and insect house. There, we visit the tanks of geckos, iguanas, bearded dragons, and rat snakes. Like a magnet, I am drawn to the exotic butterfly wall. Blue Morphos, Goliath Birdwings, and Giant African Swallowtails, their majestic wings pulled open to full span and pinned there, captive art against black velvet boards, behind dusty glass panes.

Dad and I read the names aloud, debating which is prettiest, most like the *papillon* he thinks I am. When we turn to go, Mom isn't here, and we find her sitting on the ground outside, knees up, crown petals at her feet, weeping.

The Hager Planetarium is magical in the gray-purple dusk. To the Prom Committee's credit, the trees along the path down to the main building are strung with pink lanterns and tiny green and gold lights, giving the grounds an even more romantic feel.

Max lets go of my hand, reaches into his jacket pocket, and retrieves a small silver flask. He takes a swig, and offers it to me, but I'm already buzzed, so he passes it to Bo, who drinks and passes it to Dean.

Midway down the cobblestone walkway, Max says, "Hold up," so I do, but those guys ignore him, cutting across the grass and disappearing behind the main rotunda.

"They're not going in?" I ask.

"Guess not," he says, and my heart sinks. I got all dressed up to spend the night behind some building drinking and smoking weed. But Max says, "Okay, let's do this." I look up at him, questioning, and he says, "I told you, Jailbait, I'm here to show you off, and that's exactly what I'm going to do. I have no intention of following those bozos, or making this anything but a perfect night for my girl." And with that, every fear I've had crumbles and disperses into the lilac-scented air.

Inside is a different story, and a new surge of panic

rises to my chest. People are surprised to see Max Gordon here—and me with him. People know we're dating, but it's clear from the whispers no one thought we would ever come to prom.

Max takes another swig from the flask and pulls me onto the dance floor. We dance awkwardly, and I have to work hard not to care who's watching, but the floor is crowded, so we can't do much more than move our bodies a little side to side anyway. Eventually Max takes my hand and leads me away and toward the main entrance. "Enough of that bullshit, let's take a walk," he says, and I follow, relieved, out into the balmy June night air.

Halfway up the stone path, the same one I walked with my father, his large sandals clomping against the cement, I say, "When I was little I used to come here all the time with my parents." I shake the image of rose petal crowns and Mom folded in tears by the side of a building. "I wonder if they'll be okay when my father gets home."

Max turns to me in the darkness. "Probably not," he says. "I don't mean to be a downer, Jailbait. Just realistic. I'm not sure people were meant to be burdened with family, chained down to one person forever."

"As in, married?" I ask, trying not to let his words crush me. But what if he's right? What if we're not meant to stay with only one person?

"Yeah, as in. Now, in love and fucking like rabbits? That's another story," he says, wrapping his arms around me, and pulling me to his chest. "A whole different story. Realistic *and* enjoyable."

"At least there's an in-love part," I say, trying not to choke on the rest, which seems to mix with the cloying scent of roses here, strong and sweet in the dense, humid air.

When we finally reach the top of the hillside and the wall where Mom once picked wreath grass, we stand, staring out over the vista, taking in the golden glow of moonlight rippling across the surface of the Sound.

Max moves behind me and presses his hips against me, his chin resting in the space between my neck and shoulder.

"So, how about that fucking I was talking about?" My heart speeds up, but he adds, "This will be us—can be us—every single night in California. View included."

I turn to face him. "Not here, though, right?"

"Not unless you want it to be, Jailbait."

He lets go of me, and leans out over the stone wall. He pulls the flask out, takes a sip, and hands it to me. This time, I take a big gulping swallow, and immediately double over, coughing.

"God, what is that?" I ask, when I can talk past the burning in my throat.

"Absinthe." He laughs. "It's deadly. You'd better not have more than a few sips."

He takes another, but I'm pretty sure I'm out. Already the swift burn has moved from my throat to my chest to my fingers, filling up every open space in my body.

I move closer to him, take his hand. "You know I can't wait, right? To finish exams and leave? We'll be on the road for my sixteenth birthday," I say ticking off the items I've counted so many times in my head. "There's still plenty of money left, so a nice hotel. Room service, even." I take a deep breath, trying to steady myself.

"Sixteen, huh?" he says, capping the flask and returning it to the depths of his pocket. "I barely remember sixteen."

"Really?"

"No, not really. I remember it well. It's the last time my mother came home. It wasn't pretty."

"I'm sorry, Max. I get that."

"I know you *think* you do." He peels off his jacket and

lays it across the stone wall, and jumps up onto the wall next to it. "It's a fucking sauna out here tonight," he says.

"Max—" I reach up and hold on his pant leg.

"I'm fine." He pulls away and spreads his arms wide. "'One flower, holding to the cliffs, yawning at a canyon . . .'"

"What?" I call up. He looks down at me and laughs.

"Kerouac. 'One flower, holding to the cliffs, yawning.' Something like that. I forget. You should read him. Get to know him. Your nana should have married him." He jumps back down and wraps his arms around me. "Fuck that. I'm drunk, and he was out of his mind. You should marry me."

He reaches into his pocket and gets down on one knee, and holds out a red piece of tissue paper.

"What is this, Max?" The air spins for real now. For a second, I wonder if I'm dreaming.

"I didn't have a nice box or anything. I should have gotten a box. I'm not so great at making things pretty."

"You didn't have to get me anything." But he's laughing and my head is swimming with formless, amoebic thoughts, the smell of lilacs and roses suddenly so pungent in my nose, they're making me nauseous. I peel the paper back. A delicate gold ring with a filigree butterfly on it, with blue enamel-glazed wings, winks up at me in the moonlight.

"It's a Morpho, right?" he asks, and I nod, speechless and a little bit terrified because what if he's actually proposing to me? But it's so very beautiful I could cry. Also, my tongue isn't working and maybe my throat has swelled, and I feel like I can't breathe. "According to the lady in the shop, it's an antique. Eighteen-karat gold," he says, slipping it on my finger.

And then he's singing, and the flask is out again and I'm drinking even though I shouldn't, and we're on the ground, and his lips are on my neck, then my chest, and my voice, breathless, is saying, "Max, I want to," and the earth reels out from under me as he hikes up my dress, and his pants are down, and my undersides are wet with damp from the dew.

And as he pulls his underwear down, I hear myself say, "Oh god, don't," but it's not because I don't want to, and it's not even to him, but to me. The absinthe rushes my throat, and I'm rolling away from him, my guts spilling up out onto the ground.

Rising up out of me, again and again and again.

Max says, "Shit! Fuck! Sorry, Jailbait. Come on. It's okay. It's all my fault. Let it come out. Get it over with. You'll feel better when it's out of you."

And then, even though I thought I had nothing left, I'm retching into bushes, the awful vinegar smell of puke blanketing everything.

The sky comes and goes, the music from elsewhere crescendos and disappears altogether, and Max comes into focus, but blurs into nothingness again.

Finally, he's there, somewhat solid, coaxing me up, telling me we have to walk, and the sensation of being dragged, of my feet crunching gravel even though I can barely move on my own.

The light intensifies, and we're in the parking lot, and people can see. Someone moves out of our way.

"Oh god, gross, look at her dress."

"This is why you don't invite sophomores to prom."

And, Max, barking obscenities, squeezing my shoulders and whispering, "Don't worry, Jailbait, we'll get you cleaned up before you get home."

And then the buses are in front of us, and the cars and the limos, and Max is still there next to me, holding me up, holding me tight, and steering me forward to our limousine.

Somewhere in there I hear Dean's voice, and Angie and Melissa asking if I'm okay.

And when Max says, "Does she look it?" one of them stifles a laugh and the other doesn't bother, just busts out laughing.

LATE JUNE
TENTH GRADE

I awaken at 3:00 a.m. to get some water and Advil, the sour taste of vomit in my mouth, and the reality of my mother, sprawled on the living room sofa, in a hot-pink kimono, surrounded by books and letters and wine, keeping me from falling back to sleep.

I pad across the room to study her. There must be five letters strewn across the table, waiting to be mailed to no one in the morning.

I pick one up.

My dearest Jack.

And another.

My dearest Jackie.

The words blur, and I wonder if I'm still buzzed from the absinthe.

I'm writing you one last time to say goodbye.

I swallow back the rising bile, and cover her with the crocheted blanket Nana made for us years ago, before tossing the letters in the bathroom wastebasket and stumbling back to bed.

Four hours later, I roll out of bed, sidestep the rancid blue dress that lies in a heap on my floor, and stare at myself in the mirror. I look like death. I'm an actual case study for why prom is held on a weeknight.

I grab the dress and ball it in a towel. I'll figure it out later. Wash it on the hand-rinse cycle, or sneak it to the dry cleaner's.

In the bathroom, I step in the shower and leave the water as cold as I can stand it. The reek of the night rinses from me, replaced with the crisp, fresh scent of green apple. Details reel back to me in sharp color: The dancing. The absinthe. Max on his knee, doing what?

I glance down at my naked fingers, wondering.

Me on the ground with my dress up. Max over me, pants down.

Me, puking.

I turn to the stream, mouth open, and swallow down gulps of cold water, trying to rinse away the awful, sour taste that lingers. When I step out and grab a towel, I see the crush of letters in the wastebasket.

Mom, on the couch.

The empty wine bottles.

At least I escaped *her* scrutiny.

Back in my room, the top of my nightstand is empty. I slide open the drawer—memory flashing—and see the small blue-butterfly ring he gave me.

Antique store. Eighteen-carat gold, he had said.

My eyes go to the other side of my room, to the drawer with the remaining bills in purple paper, a much smaller stack. At least he used some of it for me.

I pull on shorts and a T-shirt, grab my cell phone and a stale granola bar from a box that has been in there for a century, and head out the door for my final. By the time I reach the end of our street, there's a text from Aubrey:

Hey, how was prom?

Text photos!

Anyway, chem final going to be brutal.

Slumber-study party tonight at my house. You're still invited.

Girlpower = brainpower! Please come!

I twist the ring on my finger and breathe for a minute, nausea mixing with exhaustion.

I don't think I can manage more exams alone.

What time? I type. *I'll be there.*

In my gut, I know it's a bad idea, but it may be my only chance at passing.

I stand at the base of Aubrey's driveway, deciding.

Her words fade on my screen, and I have to press the home key to make them come back again. I'm rereading for some proof to trust her, or otherwise some warning not to go in.

Girlpower = brainpower! Please come!

And the note that came after I said okay:

Awesome! See you at 7. Bring pj's!

Her words seem sincere, like she means them.

Yet something feels off. Wrong. Or maybe it's that I left Mom such a mess. Or that Max seemed needy and annoyed with me.

"It's Friday night, Jailbait, and I'm a free man. What am *I* going to do all alone?"

I should go home.

Tend to Max.

Tend to Mom.

Instead, I walk up her driveway.

My hand shakes as I reach out.

I close my eyes, and ring the bell.

"Come here, Jailbait!"

Max yells from where he stands in the parking lot, waiting, next to his dirt bike, helmet in hand. I pull the ring from my pocket and slip it back on my finger. I almost forgot it was in there.

"I'm going to Aubrey's," I say, when I reach him. "Overnight. To study. I have to study, Max, and fast. Otherwise, I'm going to fail."

He pulls me to him, enthusiastically. "Fuck the final, gorgeous. Blue Morpho is fixed. Mint condition. Amazing. Wait'll you feel her. She practically hums, thanks to you. Whenever you're ready, we hit the road."

"Max—"

"What?" He holds me back and studies my face. "But, it's Friday night, Jailbait, and I'm a free man. What am *I* going to do?"

"You have to graduate first," I say, exasperated. "And I have to at least pass this class."

"Okay, fine," he says, pouting. "Do what you have to. But let me at least give you a ride home."

LATE JUNE
TENTH GRADE

"Markham, *you're* here?" Ethan stands at the door, smiling. The sentence is a question, the emphasis clearly on the "you're."

"Yeah, hey," I say, shouldering my backpack, and shoving my cell phone into my pocket. "It's me. Surprise!" I make goofy jazz hands, and offer a weak smile back. Inside, my stomach roils. I'm still a mess. I haven't eaten enough and have had too many cups of coffee.

"Well, come on in. I told you those bozos would come around." He winks, and nods to the stairs that lead up to Aubrey's room.

I freeze. The faint giddy sound of girls laughing drifts down to me.

"Actually," I say, "maybe this was a bad idea. I left my mother and . . . I'm not sure now. I think she needs me at home."

After Max drops me off, I find Mom upset, pacing, in a bright tangerine kimono. My brain rapid fires scenarios:

She talked to Dad.

He's not coming.

She's not okay.

She'll never be okay.

She needs help.

Fuck it. I can't deal with this. I need to wash puke out of a chiffon dress, and pack up my stuff for Aubrey's.

I need a quick nap.

I need to shower and get out of here.

I said I'd come.

I can't study for this final alone.

I walk past Mom, to my room, where my breath catches as soon as I open the door.

It shouldn't matter.

I shouldn't care.

I shouldn't be devastated, but I am.

The last of the butterflies are dead.

"Stay, JL. You should stay. Relax," Ethan says. "Trust me, all of this is going to seem like nothing soon."

Ethan, who has kissed my lips, who wanted me so badly. Ethan, who left without another word.

He stands watching me—eyes, what? Pleading? Sorry? Caring?—a limp slice of pizza in one hand.

"Here, give me this. You take that. Let me help." He pulls my backpack from my shoulder, leaving me with my duffel bag, and motions me inside.

"Jean Louise? Jean Louise!"

I open my eyes. Wipe my mouth. My mother is standing at my bedroom door.

Shit! What time is it?

From this angle, I only see part of her, her perfect, orange-silk-clad torso at my door.

I let my gaze drift up.

Her expression is strange. Her face, tear-stained. "Your father called," she says. "Everything is wrong. Everything is dead. Everything is screwed up and sad."

I try to focus, sit up to argue, but she's right. It doesn't matter what he said. Everything *is* screwed up. Even when I'm happy, I feel bad.

Nothing is simple.

Nothing feels okay.

And I can't remember a time when it did.

Mom walks over and strokes my hair, but I push her away.

"I'm going to Aubrey's," I say, getting up. "Me and some other girls, we're going to study. I have a chem final. I won't be back until tomorrow."

She reaches out again, to touch my hair, but I brush past her, start shoving clothes into my duffel bag.

"You're a good girl, Jean Louise," she says, as I locate my textbook and laptop, and zip those into my backpack. "I'm not right, but you are. I don't know what I did to deserve you."

I walk like a robot to the stairs. Ethan returns my backpack and I slowly start up them.

"Hey, JL?" he calls after me.

"Yeah?"

"Holler if you need me. I'm here."

FIFTEEN MINUTES EARLIER

Halfway between Aubrey's house and home, I sit on a curb, and pull out my cell phone. My bags are heavy, and I'm sweating.

"Siri, call Dad," I say, and before I can change my mind, it's ringing, and I'm racing through details I've practiced a hundred times.

It rings and rings, until: "You have reached Tom Markham of VigorVit California. Please leave a message and I'll get right back to you."

"Hi, Dad. It's me. I need to tell you some stuff."

I get up again and start walking, hoping the motion will mask the reason for my shaking voice, squinting against the waning sunlight that streaks down through the sugar maples, blinding my eyes. When I was little, they'd drop their propeller-shaped keys in droves on the cusp of summer and we would have contests to see who could catch the most mid-spiral before they touched down.

"So, here's the thing. I'm not sure when you're coming home . . . but Mom . . . Mom isn't okay, and, like, well, you should have known that, right? I mean, you *do* know that, don't you? And you shouldn't have . . ." My voice chokes up, and I fight tears. I'm filled with rage, suddenly, at him, at Nana, at everyone. "Anyway, she says you're coming home soon, but who knows? I've heard that line before. So, I'm telling you now, Dad, something isn't right. I can't stay here alone with her. Not anymore.

"So, I'm coming there, okay? You told me I could before . . . So maybe it's my fault I haven't listened. Anyway, I'm flying in and I'm gonna stay with you, until you come home. I have one more test, and then Max graduates, and I'm done for the year."

I swallow hard at my mention of Max, but I need to do that. Dad knows a little about him, but not much. I have to at least plant some seeds. I'll deal with the fallout later.

I make the left onto Aubrey's street, and glance at my watch. Twenty after seven.

"So, that's it, Dad. I'm sleeping out tonight, at Aubrey's, but please call me tomorrow. And don't discuss this with Mom. Not yet. Please understand, you haven't seen her lately. She's not good. I'll look up flights, and give you times. I'll make all the plans. And get Nana to watch her while I'm gone. Okay, thanks. I love you."

I hang up, and shove my phone away.

That's it. I did it.

One step closer to done.

At the top of the stairs, my heart starts beating too fast again. How did it come to be that I'm scared walking into my best friend's room?

Aubrey's house feels both strange and familiar. I know every room by heart. Every closet. Every nook and corner.

To my right, closest to the steps, is Mr. and Mrs. Andersson's room with the cherrywood sleigh bed, hardwood floors, and the blue-and-white toile wallpaper. "French countryside," Mrs. Andersson once told me, a pattern of trees and hills, old-fashioned families picnicking, and boys in hats walking sheep.

Their door is open, the hall quiet. Ethan's door, across from it, closed.

He always did like his privacy, even when he didn't give Aubrey the same consideration.

"Lock the door, JL," she says, pulling Mary Lennox to her bed. "We can't put it past Ethan to come barging in."

I have an overwhelming desire to peek in, smell his fresh ocean scent mixed with cocoa butter sunscreen, on the blankets, on the pillows, on his rug. Embedded in the air that belongs to him.

"Can I, JL?"

I nod, and whisper, "Anything, Ethan," and he opens my towel, and it falls to the ground.

I draw a ragged breath and let my mind shift to Max's room instead, dark and woody like he is, to his rock posters, his guitar. To the plaid bedspread, and curtains he made himself. And I'm slammed with guilt. Guilt for brushing him off. For feeling embarrassed about him around Ethan.

Guilt for longing for Ethan the way I still do.

Enough about Ethan.

I'm here to study. And I'm lucky to have Max. He's the only one who ever stuck by me.

Max loves me.

At least, I think he does.

And in a few short days, I'm leaving with him.

I up my pace, move toward Aubrey's room, my stomach clenched, my heart beating overtime.

Right outside Aubrey's door, I stop. The three of them are in there, chattering happily. Giggling. Settled. It's not even 7:30. How long ago did they get here?

Nobody is missing me. Nobody cares if I'm here. After years of being best friends, I'm only someone to feel sorry for. Out of place and unwanted.

But Aubrey's trying. *She* came to me. *She* texted. I told her I'd do this, so there's no way I'm leaving now. Maybe I'll tell her about prom, about Max and the ring, about my plans to go to California. And we'll be Aubs and JL, like always.

I look in and freeze again. All three of them sit on Aubrey's moss-green carpet. They're dressed in pajama pants and camis, heads bowed down, oblivious. Meghan and Aubrey have their backs to me, Niccole is painting Meghan's toenails, leaving Aubrey to paint her own.

"Hey," I say, softly, and a second time louder, so they can hear me over the music.

Niccole's eyes dart up, and Aubrey twists around.

"JL!" Aubrey puts the brush top back in the bottle, and holds her leg up. "I'd get up and hug you, but . . ." She waves her foot at me, a tissue weaved between her toes to separate them. "I'm so glad you made it. Did you get pizza before you came up?"

I shake my head, and move into the room, trying to ignore my pounding heart. Trying to ignore the look I see pass between Meghan and Niccole.

"Not hungry, thanks. But yeah, I'm here. You told me to come, so I did." I drop my duffel bag down near the bed, and my backpack on it, and walk to her desk where the polishes are. "Are there any good colors left for me?"

Aubrey's whole room used to be purple. Purple curtains, lavender rug, purple canopied bed.

At the end of middle school, she told her parents that no respectable high schooler could have a purple room, and now, except for the rows of dolls standing stock-still on their white-painted shelves, the room looks like it's off the glossy pages of a Pottery Barn summer catalogue. Palest blue walls, whitewashed desk, dresser, and daybed, with scalloped shells etched into the wood. I helped her design it right down to the rug.

I grab a bottle of bright blue polish with green sparkles called Mermaid's Tail and sit down next to the girls.

"So . . ." Aubrey says, when I am barely through my first toe. "Dish. We're all jealous. You know we want to hear about prom."

"*Need* to hear," Niccole says.

"We hear it was totally wild," Meghan adds.

I flush hot red. "It was good," I say, trying not to sound defensive. Maybe they're genuinely interested. *Or maybe they're baiting me.* "I'm still a little tired. I may have gotten a little too drunk by mistake." I need to head off whatever they might know.

"By mistake," Meghan repeats, and Aubrey's eyes shift to her sharply.

"No, I get it. I've had that happen," Niccole adds quickly.

I concentrate on my toenails, but can feel them watching me. Finally, I say, "Anyway, it was good. Fun. I crashed when I got home today, which is why I was late."

"Ah," Meghan says, and Aubrey glares at her again.

I wave my feet around to dry the polish, then get up and walk over to the three-tiered shelves that hold Aubrey's doll collection, each one staring out, dusty and dated, frozen in time.

There must be thirty of them lined up in their costumes from around the world. Mexico. Panama. Cuba. Finland. Zimbabwe. Whenever Aubrey's parents or a relative or family friend traveled out of the country, they always brought one back for her.

I had memorized some of their names and traditional costume pieces. Lana, the Tahitian doll with her wild hair, coconut bra, and headdress and skirt made of fake grass and shells and flower petals. The African doll, Eshe, with her bright-colored beaded wrap, her headdress and *idzilla* necklaces, holding a mbira in her hand. Magdalena from Madrid, her ruffled flamenco dress, large red flower in her hair, and tiny castanets that really worked if you clicked them together with your fingers.

Magdalena was Aubrey's favorite, even though she had three large cracks down her pretty porcelain face from when Ethan threw a Super Ball at Aubrey during some dumb fight they were having. Luckily, the ball missed Aubrey's head, hitting Magdalena instead, sending her toppling to the floor, her face shattering into several horrifying pieces. Ethan got punished, and Mr. Andersson spent a whole afternoon supergluing her back together as best he could. You could still see the thin black lines running through her.

"Come on back, J.L. You need a second coat." Aubrey waves the bottle of Mermaid's Tail in my direction. "Then we'll get studying. Promise." She crosses her heart, but she's concerned. Or maybe annoyed. I'm not sure.

Maybe it's the dolls. Maybe they remind her of Mary Lennox, of our stupid, childish escapades. The last time I saw Mary Lennox was at the end of middle school, when I opened Aubrey's closet to borrow a dress and saw her shoved in the back like some doll out of a horror movie.

"She's creepy in there," I had told Aubrey, "like that Chucky doll or something. You should just give her away."

Aubrey had shrugged, making me wonder if she still used her the way we used to, but was afraid to admit it. But that was back then when we could still pretend that well.

I walk back over and sit down, present my toes to her for a second coat. "Here, you do it for me," I say.

"What color is that?" Meghan asks.

"Mermaid's Tail."

"Nice," she says. She holds her fingers out toward Aubrey and me, her short nails polished a dark burgundy, the color of dried blood. "Mine is Black Cherry. Do you like it?"

"It's okay," Aubrey says.

"What about you, JL? Maybe Aubs is right. A little too slutty or goth? I should add some of Niccole's sparkle pink on top. Toss it, Nic."

I try to ignore the panic starting to build back up in my chest. Niccole tosses the bottle of pink sparkle coat to Meghan, who says, "Maybe JL needs the cherry more, right?"

Aubrey gives her a look.

"What?" she says. "I'm strictly talking polish here. Get your mind out of the gutter."

"Sorry, she's just teasing," Niccole says, and Aubrey reaches out and squeezes my fingers, but my stomach twists with the overwhelming desire to go home.

"Come on. Let's study," Aubrey says.

We quickly come up with a system, deciding to go chapter by chapter, each taking fifteen minutes to read before discussing, then doing the sample questions at the end of the unit together. We manage this for about an hour before it becomes clear that, despite Max and prom and all the distractions with my mother, I actually know this stuff better than I thought, and way better than the other girls.

Which is when it occurs to me:

This is the reason they invited me.

Not because they like me. Not because they want me. Not because Aubrey misses me. But because I can explain covalent bonds.

Aubrey looks up and asks, "Hey, JL, how are the butterflies?"

"That's right," Niccole adds. "Aubrey says you raise butterflies. That's cool. I went to one of those exhibits once, at the Museum of Natural History."

"The Conservancy," I say.

"Yes, that. They had a special exhibit. And, oh my god, there were these freakishly giant, lime-green butterfly things, with these long . . ." She motions with her hands like she's making a tail, and shudders.

"Not butterflies. Luna moths," I say.

"Yes, those. Wow, you're good. You know your stuff, don't you? But if one of those landed on me at night . . ." She shudders again.

Aubrey yawns. "Ugh. All this chem is making me sleepy. Let's go through our individual notes instead." She gives a look to both girls and adds, "See if someone has something we forgot to write down."

We open our notebooks. Aubrey glances at mine and says, "Let's start with JL's notes. I told you hers would be better than ours." Her face reddens because her motives are obvious. She knows, and I know. "It's just, your notes are always awesome, JL. I told these guys you wouldn't let a little romance interfere with your schoolwork. I bet your notes could beat ours in your sleep." She smiles, but my skin is crawling. ". . . We do, don't we, Niccole?"

Niccole nods, but I've missed what she's agreeing with. I can't hear through the sound of blood banging, angry, in my ears.

"Do what?" I ask, starting to feel sick.

"Admire you, of course," Aubrey says.

"Definitely," Niccole agrees, causing Meghan to roll her eyes.

Niccole jumps up. "Oh, hey, I almost forgot!" She pulls a brown paper lunch bag out and dumps an array of candy bouncing onto Aubrey's rug. Smarties, Sugar Babies, Dum Dums, Tootsie Pops, Jolly Ranchers.

"Is that from *Halloween*?" Meghan flicks away a Tootsie Roll that's landed on her foot.

"So what? Candy doesn't go bad." She sticks a grape lollipop in her mouth. "Oh my god. So much better," she says, slurping between words.

"You and your oral fixation," Meghan says.

"Who doesn't have one of those?"

"You got that right. Right, JL?" Niccole winks at me, and tosses an orange Tootsie Pop in my direction.

I toss it back and take a cherry instead. "Thanks, not a fan of orange," I say.

"Sorry. I should have guessed cherry since you already know how many licks it takes to get to the center of one."

"Niccole!" Aubrey kicks her hard, and Niccole winces.

"Don't bother, Aubrey," I say. "Let's just get it over with, since your friends clearly have something they want to say. Something way more urgent than molecular structures and chemical bonding."

"Who, me?" Niccole bats her eyelashes. "Anyway, aren't they kind of the same? Both a form of chemical bonding?" She laughs at her dumb joke. "But since you brought it up—Oh, come on, Aubrey, you know you want to know just as bad as we do. We can't help it. Stories are flying. You should set them straight. About you and Max and various states of *undress* last night?" She fans herself with her hand, and lowers her voice conspiratorially. "We want to hear *all* the gory details. I mean, we're all friends here, right?"

"Cut it out, Niccole," Aubrey says. "JL, why don't you name the characteristics of a covalent bond? Lower melting point and electrical conductivity, what else?" She's frantically trying to save us from total derailment. But it's too late and she knows it.

"Or what about the difference between polar and non-polar bonds?" Aubrey shoves her notebook at me without noticing that there's a big red circle drawn around the word "non-polar," and the words "Ask J.L." written next to it.

"Don't you mean *bi*polar?" Meghan says.

Aubrey throws her notebook and jumps up. "Jesus, Meghan, seriously! You promised!" Her face reddens and her eyes fill with tears, and it all becomes crystal clear. They've not only talked about Max and me, but Aubrey has told them about my mother.

My depressed, disassociating mother.

My sight blurs with tears. I shove my books and laptop into my backpack, and get up, my brain fighting what to say. The fury is making me dizzy, making my throat burn.

"Come on, JL, please stay. She didn't mean anything."

I turn and glare at her, but no words come. I don't care about them. It's *Aubrey* who has betrayed me.

"I need to use the bathroom," I say.

I lock the door behind me, and sit on the toilet trying to breathe. When I've collected myself, I walk to the sink and stare hard at my face in the mirror.

Did I do something to deserve this?

I've fooled around with Max, but not everything, and I did it because I wanted to. Is it wrong to do stuff with a person you love? I am not the first tenth grader who has ever been with a guy. I've heard plenty of stories about girls who have done plenty of things, and I've never judged them.

Maybe they don't know what it's like to be in love. So in love that being with that person fully is the only thing you want, the only thing you think about.

Maybe Aubrey doesn't know, but I do.

And Max does.

And that's all that matters, isn't it?

I pull my phone from my pocket and text Max—Heading home, come hang out?—and wait for him to respond, but nothing comes through. He's probably out riding with Dean and Bo, or in the garage working on Blue Morpho.

I'll go home and wait for him there.

I splash cold water on my face to wash away the tears and, feeling a stronger resolve, walk back to Aubrey's room. I don't need those girls any more than they need me.

A few feet from her door I stop. I can hear them talking about me.

"Come on, Aubs," Meghan is saying, "A slut is a slut is a whore. You said so yourself. You don't want to be associated with that."

"She's not a slut."

"Well, she's not a virgin, either. You can tell from the way she walks. Seriously, I'm not making it up. That's what happens when a guy like Max Gordon does you over and over again."

"You're being gross," Aubrey says. "You don't even know what you're talking about."

"I do, too. Ask Ethan. You said you think she fooled around with him."

I feel dizzy again, like I'm going to pass out.

I just need to get my stuff and go home.

"JL . . ." Aubrey says, when I step in the room. "Forget what she said. She doesn't know what she's talking about."

Hot tears sting my face. Aubrey turns to me, helpless. She knows she betrayed me. Whatever I do next is her fault.

I walk to her closet, calmly, and open the door. I reach back into the dark recesses until I feel Mary Lennox. I grab that stupid doll out by her hair.

I throw her on the bed and yank her dress up, and glare at Aubrey, my heart banging too loud in my ears.

"There," I say, tears spilling. "Why don't you tell these girls what a saint you are? What you taught me to do with her. 'Here, JL, it's only a game. It feels good. Do it. Try it,'" I say, my voice rising. "'I won't tell if you won't.' Go on, Aubs. Why don't you show them how you like to hump your stupid doll?"

"JL—" Aubrey's voice is so heartbroken, I can barely stand to hear it. But I can't stop myself, either. The fury of the past few months is a runaway train, jumping the tracks, and hurtling over a cliff now.

"Go on, Aubs," I demand. "Show them. Since you're so hard up, I'm sure you still do." I hurl the doll at her, and she lands obscenely, with one leg straddled in the air. I grab my bags, stopping at her door.

"Oh, and the two of you? You're sad, and boring, and pathetic. Speaking of Ethan, ask him. He thinks so, too."

I slam her bedroom door behind me and fly down the stairs, and past the kitchen, not turning around, fumbling at the front door that has long since been locked for the night.

"Hey, Markham, is everything okay?"

I whirl around. "Fuck you, Ethan! No, really!" I need every single Andersson to leave me alone.

I yank the door open, and stumble with my things out into the dark.

"JL, wait! Stop. Please." Ethan follows me. "Slow down. Tell me what happened. Let me help."

"You want to help?" I yell, turning back. "You want to help! Maybe don't feel me up in the bushes, then leave for school and act like I never existed! How's that for helping? How about you don't act like I matter, when everything that's ever happened shows I sure as hell don't!"

"JL!" he calls, as I step off the curb. "Of course you matter. Of course you do! Come back! Talk to me. I'm worried about you."

"Well, it's a little late for that, so don't be!" I yell behind me, and disappear down the street, into darkness.

The cold shocks me. Somewhere in the back of my mind, I know this is crazy. It's June, so I shouldn't be shaking like I am.

But I am. My whole body is trembling.

Fuck Aubrey. Fuck Ethan.

I don't need his help, or anyone's.

To hell with all of them.

My mother and father, too.

I don't need anyone but Max.

And then, this idea:

We should go tonight!

Why not?

It's completely perfect.

I'll tell Max. He'll agree. He won't care.

To hell with school. With graduation.

We'll go tonight.

We'll go tonight!

Figure out how to fix everything later.

I'm practically running by the time I reach the street before ours. At least I'm not shaking anymore.

In case he hasn't gotten my other message yet, I fish my phone from my pocket and text Max again:

Change in plans. Pack for CA. Bring Blue Morpho. I want to leave now!

By the time I reach our street, the air is blanketed in pitch blackness. *What time is it?* I glance at my phone. It's already 10:00 p.m.

So what? We can get started. Go a few hours and stay the night in a hotel.

I reach home and run up the damp lawn, my brain flying with delirious thoughts I can't even begin to nail down.

What to pack? What to leave?

I don't need much. Just some shorts and a few T-shirts, and the rest of the money. My phone and my laptop. Whatever I can fit in a backpack. I can't exactly bring a suitcase on a motorcycle. I never even thought about that. I'll call Nana from the road in the morning. I'll give Dad some bogus flight times tomorrow.

And Mom? I can lie: *I forgot something I needed for Aubrey's and came home for it. Max is here to give me a ride back.*

It's all falling into place.

It's all falling into place.

In less than an hour, we can be out of here.

I stumble in the darkness, wondering why the outside lights haven't gone on. Or maybe Mom turned them off. Maybe she's already gone to bed.

The house is dark, too. Only the soft blue glow of the television through the living room window. She probably fell asleep on the couch again.

I slip my key from my pocket and open the front door. The television murmurs softly in the background.

"Scrub with one side, gently brush away dirt with the other . . ." Some infomercial, hawking a miracle sponge.

I turn to close the door, quietly. Only then do I notice Blue Morpho.

Max is here already! He got my message! That's why he isn't responding.

He must have gotten my first text and beat me here.

My thoughts reel a little, twist back on themselves in knotted circles. But I can't pay attention to them. Not now. Max is here, and I want to go, and yet my limbs feel laden and exhausted.

Of course they do. All of it, prom, Aubrey's, finals, everything has sapped me of energy. When did I have a good night's sleep last? I wonder briefly if I have time to nap before we leave.

"Max?" I call softly, moving past the living room. I don't want to wake Mom if she's sleeping.

In the kitchen, I stop. Two empty wineglasses. Two empty bottles. Max's leather jacket slung over the back of a chair.

He came early for me. Got bored.

Mom kept him company, no big deal.

He's waiting in my room, and she's gone to bed.

These are the merciful thoughts that come to me.

I know what you're thinking, Aubrey, but face it.

Sometimes we can't see what we don't want to.

"Max?" I drop my bags on the kitchen floor, and move toward the darkened hall. "Max?"

A bad thought forces its way in. *What if he came here for the rest of the money?*

But he wouldn't do that. Max isn't like that. He would wait for me. He wouldn't use me for money.

"JL!" He walks out into the hallway, confused. Squints in the dark. Rakes his hands through disheveled hair. "What are you doing here? Home? I mean—"

I cut him off. I need to help him see things fast. To clarify.

"You got my text?" I smile, grateful. He's already packed, and here. Even if he's not, we can stop back at his place and get his things on the way out.

"Yeah," he says. "That."

Everything feels off. His words sound hollow in my ears. The air feels smoky and viscous, like I can't quite focus or pull in a breath.

He knew I was coming or he wouldn't be here, right?

"Right," he says, answering words I haven't spoken aloud.

I move toward him, to hug him. To thank him. To tell him it's right that we should go.

His shoes are off. He's barefoot. I can smell the sour odor of alcohol oozing from his pores.

"I want to go. Now." I lower my voice. "We'll figure the rest out later. I want to leave tonight for California, okay?"

"Okay," he says. "You do?" His expression is weird.

Scared. His posture is odd. He's not standing like he normally does.

Which room did he come from?

He's midpoint between Mom's bedroom door and mine.

"Yes. Right now," I say. The rush comes back to me, the one from the street. The sense of exhilaration. Of running free. "You brought Blue Morpho," I say.

"Right," he says. "I did." He turns and looks behind him—for what?—and turns back to me. "Your mom—" he says, but I cut him off.

"I don't care. I don't give a shit what she does. What she says."

"Okay, I have to get my shoes . . . they're in—"

"You do that," I say. I smile, but my lips stretch funny, like a cartoon clown. "I'll be right out, okay?"

"JL?"

"Yeah?"

"Are you sure?" he asks.

"Yes." I squeeze his hand, and run to my room.

See? He was waiting for me. The money is still here.

"Jackie? Where'd you go, Jackie? Come back!"

My mother's voice trails from down the hall.

I move faster. Not thinking. Not doubting. Not wanting to hear her crazy words. Simply knowing this is what we need to do. *I* need to do. To feel better. To get away from Aubrey. From her. From everything.

Just me and Max, on Blue Morpho.

It takes me less than five minutes to shove everything I need in a bag.

Part V

The Blue Morpho's vivid wings result from microscopic scales that reflect light. But the undersides are a dull brown. When it takes flight, the contrasting colors flash, making it look as if it is appearing and disappearing.

LATE JUNE
TENTH GRADE

As long as I live, I'll never be able to adequately describe the freeness of riding on the back of Blue Morpho. The cold rush of air, hair trailing back, tangled in the wind. The rhythmic vibrato of motion and sound that blocks everything else from your head.

Maybe that, alone, made everything worth it.

Or maybe nothing ever will.

But sooner or later the wind dies down, the night sky lightens from gray to mauve to coral pink and back to periwinkle again, before the sun is out, up, rising high in the sky, casting a glare so strong you have to shield your eyes against the onslaught. Gas stations call. Bathroom stops. And you realize you're not dressed properly and gravel kicks up from the road so hard it leaves angry red welts on your shins. That's when the pieces threaten to come back to you, at first like a fever dream you can write off as confusion, exhaustion, delusion, as vague and unsure as the landscapes that fly past, but eventually—eventually—so fully, so crisp and unrelenting, you have to force yourself to ignore them, dismiss them, because otherwise they will take you down.

But not yet they don't.

First the fever dream.

And before all that:

We stop at Max's house, so he can get me a helmet and gather his things.

"Don't forget the money," I remind him, though I'm not sure how much is left of what he's taken. "And be fast, okay, Max?" because even in this flustered, altered state, I understand time and daylight are my enemy.

"I won't, and I'll be as fast as I can. But I have to look out for you. You can't ride from here to California without a helmet."

I have to look out for you.

How many people say that without ever meaning it?

But Max means it. He always has.

I wait outside, on the idling, vibrating seat of Blue Morpho, the shivering threatening to return to my body, his sad, dilapidated house before me, looking even more sad and dilapidated in the darkness.

Is that yelling—the slap of hand against something hard—coming from inside?

When Max returns, it's not lost on me how cautious he seems. How concerned. As if he's reluctant, when he's the one who wanted this all along.

"Come on, Max. Please."

He nods, and squints at me, studying me for answers to questions I don't know any better than him, as he secures his bag on the back with mine by a bungee cord he loops around over and over, for what seems a hundred minutes, then runs back into the garage and emerges with the silver helmet I wear in his hand.

"You sure, Jailbait?" he asks one more time, strapping it as tightly as he can on my head. "We'll stop somewhere tomorrow and get you a better one . . . But I mean it, JL. We don't have to do this. Not yet. Not now. Maybe I'm not the best—"

I shake my head hard, press a hand to his mouth, to stop him from saying one word more.

If you've ever plugged a request for directions from Long Island, New York, to Malibu, California, into Google Maps, you'd know it's more than 2,800 miles from our coast to theirs. 43 hours by car. 263 hours by bicycle.

Nearly a thousand hours if you wanted to try to walk from here to there.

You'd be surprised what a straight shot it is. Almost directly due west on I-80, with only the slightest sweep north through the Midwest. Illinois. Iowa. Nebraska. Another sweep south when you hit Colorado.

"We could be there by Sunday night," I tell him. "Or I guess Monday if we want to rest, get a hotel room, and sleep. I'm going to have to call and talk to Dad at some point, make up some flight times. Check in with my mom."

She probably doesn't even realize I'm not at Aubrey's.

Max nods, and the thought of my nana, worried, slips through my mind. But I'll make it up to her, explain everything once I'm safe at Dad's. She once kissed Kerouac. She'll understand.

Max checks the throttle, presses the starter, shifts into first, stamps on the pedal, and the bike revs up, and we take off slowly, the terrain bumpy on the pitted back roads of his neighborhood. But soon we're on the highway, and the road evens out, and the kilter and hum of the bike grow steady.

I wrap my arms around him, close my eyes, and press my forehead to the cool leather surface of his jacket.

I hadn't realized how very tired I am.

———

Near 2:00 a.m., we stop at some deserted old gas station near the Delaware Water Gap to fill up. Max is oddly quiet, still pensive and brooding. I thought he'd be excited, over-zealous even, but mostly he just watches me, checking for something, though I'm not sure what. Maybe proof that I know what I'm doing.

I don't.

I don't have a clue what I'm doing. But it feels right. It feels like the only choice I have.

By 4:00 a.m., I'm seeing signs for Williamsport, which I think is where they have some big baseball thing my father used to talk about. "Williamsport?" I yell, because I'm hop-ing Max gives a shit. I need to talk. I'm having a seriously hard time staying awake, and it's not like you can sleep on the back of a Kawasaki.

"Nice!" Max yells back. "Little League World Series place, right?"

If Max is tired or needs a break he doesn't say so, and when I ask that next, he yells back that he's okay, how we should keep on moving.

"I'm going to need to sleep eventually!" I call to him.

Soon we're passing signs for State College, and by the time the sun is rising, I'm seeing signs for the Allegheny National Forest.

I tug on Max's shoulder, then tug harder. Every part of me feels stiff and sore from hanging on. "I have to pee!" I yell. "I have to rest. There's a sign for a motel up there."

Max doesn't answer, but he obliges.

He veers Blue Morpho off at the next exit ramp.

The Shawnee Motel may be the most pathetic, least ro-mantic place in the entire world. Its lobby sports little in the way of décor. Two threadbare blue couches, four clashing blue chairs, and walls the beige of an old ACE bandage. The place smells of dust and mildew, and a faint, sharp smell I'm hoping isn't urine, but chlorine.

"Can I help you?"

The clerk is barely a grown-up, not much older than Max. Still, I worry he'll be suspicious. Turn us away because of my age. Or, worse, report us.

Max squeezes my hand, and knocks near my pocket, and though it takes me a tired second, I pull a bill from my stash.

"We need a room for a few hours, for my sister and me," Max says. "We're on our way to Cleveland to visit our pop. We need a nap. To wash up and rest. I can pay cash if you want."

"I don't need a whole explanation," the clerk says. "Cash, credit card, I don't care. So long as you pay, you're fine."

If the lobby is depressing, the room is worse. Though it does have a balcony that looks out over a sorry, green pool and half the parking lot.

We drop our bags on the bed, and Max says he's showering. I stare at the green bedspread worn down to a sheen, and vow that my first time won't be here, not in this gross, pathetic place.

I'm too tired anyway. I'm sure Max is, too. He won't mind. He's waited this long. I'll find us somewhere nicer to stay tonight. A Marriott or a Hampton Inn. Heck, I'd rather be outside, on a blanket on the edge of some scenic overlook, than here.

I listen to the shower run, unlock the terrace door, and step outside.

What is it that makes us suddenly remember, Aubrey? What makes us take notice of what is actually around us, rather than what we want to see?

Is it a janitor at a dumpster, emptying an industrial-sized gray pail, then checking his cell phone, and muttering some obscenity at the ground?

Is it a maid pushing a metal cart from one sad motel room to the next, a stack of thin white towels folded on top?

Or is it the red Toyota that pulls into the parking lot, a pretty woman, unsteady, with long black hair getting out?

Or maybe it's not any of those, but something else, something smaller. Something simple and stupid, and momentarily sweet and soothing, but utterly jarring to the brain. The sound of your boyfriend's voice drifting out from the shower, some lame old lyrics you've never heard before, spilling out and obliterating you through a half-open bathroom door.

"*You can't sit under an orange tree*
In a grove full of thorns . . ."

Max's voice is soothing at first, slipping out with the steam through the bathroom door. It makes me laugh even, his nutjob songs with the nutjob lyrics no one my age has ever heard before.

"*You can't pick the sweet tangerines,*
When the trees to begin with ain't yours . . ."

The kind of song my mother was singing. Something dumb about loganberry pie. My mother and Max, peas in a pod. Max and his apples and his tangerines.

Tangerine.

I blink at the janitor as he disappears back through the

main entrance, and close my eyes altogether as the maid does the same into a room below me.

But open or closed, I can't make it stop. Max's voice, mixing with the details from last night. When I first came in from Aubrey's house.

Not how Max was already there.

Not the television or wine bottles.

Not the two glasses, or Max's leather jacket on the chair.

No. It's the other details. Ones I missed at first.

Because I didn't want to see.

Max, staggering, panicked. Zipping his jeans.

His T-shirt, inside out.

His feet, bare.

Shoes, I don't know where.

And something else.

Something way worse. Through the sliver of my mother's open door:

Her orange kimono, lying twisted on the floor.

That's it, Aubrey. I'm not spelling it out any clearer. It's already more than you'll ever need to know.

More than I, or anyone, ever need to know.

Yet there it is. So now you do.

Like I said when I started this thing, it's yours to keep, but, please, you can't ever tell.

It would break everything. Dad coming home and Mom getting better are all the hope I have left now.

Promise me, please, it never leaves these pages.

Promise me, Aubrey. Promise me.

So, what's left of the story, now, to tell?

Just Max.

Of course you want to know about that.

"JL?"

The air is thick. Unbreathable. Everything moves in slow motion.

Max, walking toward me. From the sad hotel room out to the balcony.

I hear him on his way, each sound, each movement, magnified.

The shower turning off.

The towel rough against his skin.

Jeans zipping.

His backpack opening, him rifling through.

He's putting on deodorant.

He's searching for things.

I can't bring myself to look at him.

"Jailbait?"

The balcony door is open. We're only two floors up. If I wanted to, I could squeeze between the bars and drop down.

If I fell and shattered, would it hurt worse than the pain I am in?

"Hey, what are you doing out—?" He stops. The tears on my face, the slump of my shoulders, tell him everything.

"I'm so sorry, Jailbait."

I hold up my hand against his words. There isn't really anything he can say.

"I need to go, Max," I say, my voice clear and forceful. "I need to get to the airport and go without you. There's a flight that leaves at six tonight, from an airport in Cleveland."

I hold my cell phone screen out to him. I've already checked the times.

"Okay," he says. He puts a hand on my shoulder, but I flinch and he takes it away. "I tried, Jailbait, I tried to, tried . . ." he stammers. "It was a mistake, and I was trying to tell you." I nod through my tears. "I was wrong, really wrong, and . . . It was too late. I didn't know what else to do."

And he was trying, wasn't he? That much is true. He had been trying, from the minute I saw him in the hall.

Certainly, once we reached his house.

"Are you sure, Jailbait?" he had pleaded. "Maybe I'm not the best—"

I had put my hand to his mouth.

I had made the admission go away.

The Cleveland Hopkins International Airport in Cuyahoga County, Ohio, is a long three hours from the Shawnee Motel in Pennsylvania. It's not even 9:00 a.m., so I tell Max to rest first. We'll make it in plenty of time.

I lie down, too, on the opposite side of the bed, and watch him sleep, his breath uneven, his eyes fluttering restlessly behind his lids.

I'm in bed with Max Gordon, but not how I planned. There's an ocean between us, and I'll never swim back to that side.

He will take me to the airport, and my father will pick me up in California.

I am almost sixteen, and still a virgin.

Whatever else he took and gave, Max Gordon will not be the one to take that from me.

Part VI

Butterflies are covered in delicate scales that rub easily off, but they're not so delicate they will die from the human touch. They are more resilient than that.

I put the pen down, but pick it up again.

I have a few more things I want to say.

Here's a weird truth, Aubrey. I keep thinking about the Tropicals, Jezebels and "little mirrors," and the things about butterflies that amaze me.

Did you know that some of the most beautiful species of butterflies on earth eat their own? The Blue Morpho, for instance, is one. You wouldn't think something that pretty would do something that terrible, yet it does.

And the Black Muted Spangle, with its velvety indigo wings, was deemed extinct by expert lepidopterists until someone rediscovered them in India. Not gone, Aubrey, only missing from human detection.

And here's a thing about butterflies that no one gets, really. We think they're so fragile. Easily harmed or worse. But they're not. Not really.

They're stronger than we give them credit for.

Take that Jezebel whose wing I fixed. She was the last Jezebel standing at the end of spring. Like how a broken bone gets stronger with the healing, maybe our bruises make us tougher in the end.

But enough about butterflies. You'll want to know what's next for me, here, on Dad's balcony in California. I'll put it this way: I don't mind if we stay a bit longer.

There's something to be said for palm trees and sea breezes.

Mom and I should have both given it more of a chance.

As for school, Dad called and explained, gave them some bastardized version of the truth that had already been bastardized by me. Not lies, exactly, but omissions.

Some things are better kept unsaid.

Whatever he told them, it worked. They gave me till the end of summer to take my chem final online. My father is good at that, isn't he? Negotiating deals. A master salesman.

And Max and me, well, that's over. And the truth is: I almost feel worse for him than me.

Almost, but not really.

Not enough to take his calls, at least.

And he does keep calling me.

Calling and texting that he's sorry.

He feels awful.

He misses me.

He loves me.

He wants me to be okay.

And there's the matter of the money. However much of it is left. He offered to send it. But, right now, I don't really care about that.

So I don't answer. I can't talk to him. I'm not ready yet.

It's not that I hate him; I don't. But it's also not the kind of thing you can easily forgive.

You were right about that part, Aubrey. There were plenty of things about Max that weren't good for me. Things I wasn't ready for. But others I was. And, at least in the end, I stood up for myself. But that doesn't mean there wasn't a price to pay.

I do get this: I was naïve about some things, and you were trying to protect me, even if you weren't sure against what.

Which reminds me. I used to watch this show with Max. I think you know it. A cartoon called <u>BoJack Horseman</u>. It's about this horse who's a washed-up actor in Hollywood, and in some episodes he dates this owl. It's stupid and ridiculous, and really funny. And at the end of Max's favorite episode, she says this thing about red flags and how, when you wear rose-colored glasses, they only look like regular ones.

So, maybe that was me. Maybe I missed the red flags because I saw Max through rose-colored glasses.

But there were things you were wrong about, too. I need to be clear. I wasn't a slut, or a whore, or a Jezebel, no matter what I did, or didn't do.

I'm just me, a sixteen-year-old girl, ready to move forward, and to feel things.

And I won't feel bad about that, Aubrey. Or bad about anything I'm ready for.

You shouldn't, either, when you are.

So, I guess that's it. I leave us here.

Where we wind up later is a mystery.

After you read this, you'll make up your mind.

But I do want you to know that I'm sorry. Sorry for hurting you. Sorry for not telling you about Ethan. Sorry for not trying harder to listen. And sorry for sharing our dumb old secret about a doll. I know what betrayal and humiliation feel like, and I wouldn't wish those things on my worst enemy. I certainly wouldn't wish them upon you.

So, I'm sorry. I hope that's enough. Enough for us to find our way back to understanding. That we can be civil . . . or something even better when I get back.

Because, yes, we're coming back. That part is true. My mom can keep baking because my father is finally coming home.

Hopefully then she'll get better. Maybe we need to find her someone better than Dr. Marsdan.

And that's it. End of story. I'm trusting you won't tell anyone. It would only hurt people for no good reason. I know my mother didn't mean it—couldn't have meant it—simply took him for some old, dead writer.

Would it be so bad to let the truth die with him? With Kerouac?

Let it be dead to all of us.

Oh, and one more thing, Aubrey. Not sure if you noticed the date, but it's officially my birthday. I turned sixteen today. Can you believe it was only a few short months ago that Nana insisted on getting me the Tropicals? She meant well, didn't she? But I can't help but wonder if things might have been different if I had stuck to the common ones, the Monarchs and brush-footed fritillaries, the garden variety I always raised, that were easy to set free in my own backyard.

I guess we'll never know.

With love and hope,
JL

I put the pen down, hand cramping, and sit breathing with the pages in my lap.

JUNE 29
SUMMER BEFORE ELEVENTH GRADE

It's less than a mile to the post office on Heathercliff Road, across from the Point Dume shopping center. I've passed it with Dad a half a dozen times since I got here, more than a week ago.

I change into my bikini—the one Nana got me with the neon butterflies that I somehow managed to throw in my backpack—and pull a sundress over that with sneakers and sunglasses. Dad took me shopping. I have no shortage of things to wear, summer clothes.

In Dad's office, I find a stamp and an envelope, and scrawl the address I know by heart across the front.

As I head out to Dume Drive, west toward Heathercliff, the sun beats down unrelentingly hopeful and bright.

By the time I reach the double glass doors of the post office, I'm sweating. My reflection in the pane takes me by surprise. I look older than I did a few weeks ago. Sophisticated and brave, glamorous, even. Like I belong in Los Angeles County, California.

Inside, the blast of air conditioning envelops me, chilling the sweat on my neck, making the hairs there prickle and stand. I lower my sunglasses so my eyes can adjust to the dim gray light of indoors, and join the line of patrons waiting for their turn.

Ahead of me are six customers, and though there are three windows, only one of them is manned. The frazzled-looking postal clerk sighs. I scan to my left, to the row of blue steel boxes, to the middle one that reads: "First Class Mail. Out of Town."

Good enough. I step out of line.

The handle is cold; the mouth of the mailbox squeaks loudly as I lower it down.

"Here goes nothing," I say, aloud, rereading the only address on the envelope, though it takes one more breath to be sure:

J.-L. Kerouac
7 Judy Ann Court
Northport, NY 55122

I smile, and let go, my words disappearing into the dark.

The sand is hot, making it hard for me to touch my bare feet to the ground. I wish I hadn't left my flip-flops back at the base of the wood stairs.

I yank my sweatshirt off, tie it around my waist, readjusting my sunglasses, which don't seem to help much against the glare.

A few yards ahead, Mom and Dad walk together toward the ocean, Mom in a flowy white sundress and straw hat, Dad in some ratty old Dylan T-shirt and khaki shorts.

His hair is getting longer again, and he wears it slicked back. I noticed this morning how it's streaked with gray.

Dad leans into Mom and says something, and Mom throws her head back and laughs. He takes her hand, and she links her fingers through his. I look away, bend down to pick up a shell. A shiny pale peach thing the color of grapefruit ices, a perfect pinprick hole in the top. Good to lace a string through, I think. I slip it in my pocket and keep walking.

Ahead of me, the ocean sparkles. Silver-white flecks of sunlight pop off its surface like soda bubbles. Overhead, gulls swoop and caw. A kite surfer dangles from a yellow-and-cobalt nylon arch.

Everything is effervescent and over-bright; dizzying, as if I'm caught in a dream.

When they reach the water's edge, Dad turns and calls to me, "You coming, JL?" But I want to stay back, here by myself, looking on.

I hold up a hand, letting them know to go on in without me.

"Suit yourself!" Dad calls, pulling my mother by the arm. When she resists, he scoops her up, throws her over his shoulder, and wades in, her hat falling off, the white of her dress blending into the frothy white foam of the surf.

A flash of memory:

A boy and a girl.

A dusty garage.

A blue bike.

Longing tugs at my chest, but I won't give in to it. Something else, soon, will take its place.

I take a few steps more down shore, to where the pale fine sand holds some dampness, and sit and watch my parents romp, going under and coming up, again and again.

In my pocket, my phone vibrates. My heart quickens, and I reach in. But I merely retrieve the jingle shell instead. I run my fingers over the smooth, cool promise of its surface.

The phone vibrates a third and fourth time before it stops.

I smile, and inhale deeply, and hold the shell up in front of me to squint at its sharp edges, careful not to block the hole with my fingers, so a pinprick of light can shine through.

ACKNOWLEDGMENTS

It gets harder and harder to write acknowledgments for so many reasons, but mostly because I'm older and more distracted, and bogged down by world events, but also because, often, so much time has gone by from the first writing of a manuscript to the publication of a book. This is not more true than for this book. In fact, I wrote the first draft more than a decade ago (though it wasn't until my extraordinary editor, Vicki Lame, read it, that it found both its wings and its heart). As such, if I have inadvertently left you out, it's not because your input didn't matter, but because my memory grows poorer, as the days chug on by.

To my early readers, who gave invaluable feedback, including Jeff Fielder, E. Collison, and Gila Cohen Shaw (who even bound it into a bookish book), and these three incredible readers who each read more iterations of this story than seems humanly possible: my mother, Ginger; Annmarie Kearney Wood; and Jess Grembos, whose notes changed everything—no, really, everything—unlocking a necessary key to making the whole story work. How is it possible, Jess, that you've been reading for me so long you are no longer my target audience's age?!?;

To LuAnn O'Hair, who has shared both my rough and polished work with her students, and provided constant and invaluable feedback and encouragement, including for this manuscript;

To Nora Raleigh Baskin, my often-writing partner, who read with great care, gave skilled feedback, and, most importantly, convinced me, just on description alone, it was a story worth telling;

To Kelly Hager, who always loved this one best, and is the most star-filled planetarium ever;

To Paul Hankins, who finally shows up in a book just as he should, as a teacher who motivates the otherwise-disenfranchised student to love books and be their best, authentic self;

To all my Facebook friends, who clicked the little red heart button each time I shared an excerpt, or who asked for more glimpses of "the butterfly book," aka "my porno YA." Here you go. I hope you swoon;

To my agent, Jim McCarthy—this is four and five together now, Jim, not bad, not bad. Thank you for always reading swiftly, for the abundance of exclamation points before you offer the needed criticism, for the feedback that is incredibly skilled, and for responding to emails on Saturdays, and Sunday evenings, even when I say it can wait until after the weekend; and for always seeing the potential in this one, even when I simply could not;

To the extraordinary Vicki Lame, who didn't just buy *a* book when she bought *The Memory of Things,* but instead truly took on a writer. *Me. THIS* writer. And, taught her the art of drinking bourbon while she was at it;

To the whole team at Wednesday Books and Macmillan, because it truly takes a book village and I'm deeply grateful: editorial, production, and copyediting: Jennie Conway, Elizabeth Curione, Eva Diaz, Barbara Wild, and Laurie Henderson; cover and interior design, Kerri Resnick and Anna Gorovoy (Oh, my, the absolute gorgeousness!!); marketing and publicity: Brant Janeway, DJ DeSmyter, and Meghan Harrington (without you my books would never find their way to readers' hands and hearts); and subrights: Chris Scheina, I have to, because I haven't stopped wondering if it was a typo and, ARE YOU KIDDING ME?!?! Also, to Alexandra Quill and Peter Janssen, in school/library/academic marketing, who have both been constant quiet champions of my work and, more important, to Peter, who was willing to lug Masterpiece to Houston AND let me be Bitsy Richwong Dubrowsky Keys. Who could ask for more than that?

And, lastly, as always, to my family: My parents, Stu and Ginger, my sisters, Paige and Laurie, and, especially, my boys, David, Sam, and Holden (and, yes, Charlie and Boogs), who support me endlessly, and fill my life with the most magnificent music and humor, far beyond my wildest dreams.